I0673090

Macky's Exam

Chameleon Love

In this novel, dispersed, are words from these featured artists and productions (and any others): Green Day, Eminem, Geto Boyz, Public Enemy, Laid Back, Glory soundtrack, Living Colour, Queen, Chubby Checker, Curious George (et al) Staind, Blind Willie Johnson, Sweeny Todd, Michael Jackson, Tool, Bobby Pickett and Gilligan's Island

Further, this project was greatly influenced by the works of Stephen King and Buena Vista Social Club.

Lastly, the mention of or reference to any and all entities and or products is not a challenge, either direct or indirect, to the trademarks or copyrights concerned.

ISBN: 978-0-6151-5704-7

this story is for Reeves. and me. I think.

this story is for f-troop.

TABLE OF CONTENTS

I

Embarking Passage

My eyes feel like they're gonna bleed/ My mouth is dry/ My face is numb/ On my own. . . here I go.   **Green Day**

CHAPTER ONE

History is not a mystery . . . not his story

P. Enemy

1. CATALYISTS

What? You pricked your thumb? Cut your skin? Hate got your life and ya don't know where to go? Yeah, I know; trapped. Need an angel? Oh trouble, trouble, constant bubble. Then the knock, knock, knock at the door and dang if it's not dandy. Bad, Bad Dandy.

Macky just wanted to be an average kid growing up with an average amount of love and affection. Then move away from home. Maybe wind up delivering packages and on occasion maybe mixing it up with a tough. Or stab people. Not too deep but deep enough to impress. One person—one girl, actually—but she didn't know him then. Still doesn't. Nor he her. It was more of the abstract of it all. Still, nothing big.

His parents thought big though. Big enough to give him over to a laboratory called EMAC. But Bad Dandy, his real mentor, was where the action was. Macky would learn at the hands and mind of Bad Dandy. Plus, Bad Dandy needed him to be somebody special. He knew Macky had it in him. But all that is later in our story.

When Macky was given, though he thinks taken, to EMAC, his soon to be mentor gave Macky someone to want. A picture of someone, actually. But he was never allowed to keep it. The picture is a little later in the story too though. First came the disappointed parents.

"I do not understand why God hath spited us with that boy, Martha. I do not know," pacing across the living room. The man doing this is Macky's father. He had expected great things from his son. The first something in the family, something like that.

"Martha, we've given him books and pencils and paper. Fine hemp paper to write an opus about his lineage and he only wants to befriend the children of the rabble. Where oh where has his middle-class morality gone?"

Martha, not stopping her knitting, "Oh George, our son is growing as strong as any boy of his age. Progress will just take awhile longer, that's all."

"Oh? And how long will that be?"

Martha stopped knitting. "Why I suppose that does not matter, for he will be gone tomorrow, yes?

"And when he comes back to us?"

"Whenever that happens, he will make us proud."

2. CATALYSITS part 2

Little O'Donnell lives in a little village in the shadow of a town down the way from nowhere. On a drizzly night the Heart of Oak Boys brought him in on a raid. Sitting on hay bales in a barn, Little O'Donnell got the low down.

"Old Man Springer's evicting three families this week: the Reillys, the O'Briens and the Farrells and them with not a place in the world ta flee ta and five wee mouths each to feed. Tonight we send the bastard a message ta tell him ta fuck off back ta his own godforsaken country." It was a long speech and O'Donnell's mind began to wander but his focus returned when the knife was put in his hand. Yeah, this was more like it; out in the fields chasing Springer's prize Aberdeen angus.

"Hock the bastard, ok? Cut the tendons at the back of his knees, alright boyo?"

When the knife pierced the hulking cow's tendon Little O'Donnell called forth shrieks as the beast fell to the earth; Little O'Donnell was now completely stiff. He adjusted his pants, withdrew the knife and plunged again.

When the Heart Of Oak Boys dragged him off to Kilmaley's Well half an hour later the blood was caked on his body and the cow was not recognizable as such. The boys had a bit of a debriefing too, which took the form of bouncing Little O'Donnell's head off the head of a gravestone a few times while he ripped male parts off the boys holding him. He felt nothing, not even amusement though he couldn't stop laughing. Finally the leader called a halt, saying that while he admired Little

O'Donnell's other-world creativity, he had his doubts about his ideological commitments.

"Time to move on, eh boyo?" Little O'Donnell did not disagree.

S happens and anyway it was time to really get serious and any place was as good as another but to hell and to fuck with the bedraggled mist over the spire of the glowering church; to hell and to fuck with the plopping procession of cattle on their way to Joe Brady's mart on Saturdays; to hell and to fuck with Bridie McGready and her mud-splattered ankles and sprawling bosom and she telling Little O'Donnell ta get ta fuckin, a dirty wee scut like he, and she riding every fucker in town. Ta hell and ta fuck with them all.

So tonight he's in another bar awaitin to listen to Lucky Time, the main attraction, the house draw, though Little O'Donnell did have to slash six in the alley to get a ticket. Actually, the first was the bingo, but he really needed to train this new knife. He didn't mind having to work this way either, there being little other work besides farming. That plus he had time to burn while waiting to see Lucky Time. The oil lamps burn dim when he is the main draw.

Lucky Time is not a tall man, standing five-eight—a few inches taller than Little O'Donnell will be when he matures. Lucky Time has stage presence as he stands at the edge of the stage. "You are a person I find boring," is what you feel when he looks at ya and so you're relieved when he looks at someone else. So much that you smile and beam.

"You're all a nice crowd, thank you for staying to the end of tonight's show," as

Lucky Time's pianist plays keys in twos, close together but softly as to not drown out Time's voice. "So here we are and I want to end with something we can all hum and snap to. Say you there, in the bad toupee, or is that your date? Right. You in the front row. Don't make me, right, you bubbie, tell me, where are you from? Ah, the coast, yeah, there's an easy and old tune about that."

Lucky Time drags the mike stand with him as he goes to lean against the piano. He stares into his pianists' eyes. "The coast, I see. The coast, yes, but I don't get out there, anymore."

At that moment he looks from pianist to audience then back to his pianist who tickles the beginning notes as the audience hears, "Missed the Saturday dance, heard they crowded the floor, couldn't bear it without you, don't get around much, anymore." The crowd claps at the break before the next stanza and he smiles, "stop that," then sings "thought I'd visit the club . . ." They're hypnotized.

Lucky Time is wearing a nine-inch Aquarius medallion from his gold plated rope chain. Chest hair stretching out from his upper neck to the bottom of his stomach. Stubble on his face. His shirt is sexily unbuttoned to reveal lent in his navel. Silky blue plumbed shirt. Sweat drenches it, making it shine. Tight black satin pants with a sock in the crotch and leather demi-boots. He always keeps his face away from the audience unless he's cutting or getting ready to cut them. They like it. Lucky Time wears a pinky ring and sings in that melodious tone professional gurgle drunks do when they are summoned by the boss. His straight blue-black hair is in his eyes but he's smiling with those large lips. The corners of it reach his black eyes.

"Awfully different without you, don't get around much anymore, awfully different without you, don't get around much anymore. Thank you and goodnight." The four members of the audience leave. Except for O'Donnell, who stays for another lesson from his mentor. Lucky Time leads him to the bar as the pianist leaves with a mallet in her gloved hands. "Listen boyo, you gotta win'em over in the first two minutes. That's all ya git! After that you might as well schlep them up Mount Goya! Dig me?"

"Yeah, yeah, right. Gosh, I can't wait to be like you."

"Well, you have been picked but you still must convince the suits that you can run things. Remember, this assignment is your last trial before complete lunacy. But stop trying to erect a killing school; ya no teacher. Remember that Ronald fellow? He became a pervert, so just convert the one that goes by the name Macky. He's the last one for you but you're behind schedule and it will not look good if he shucks his duty again. You must turn him into a killer. The girl, well she's fine but the boy, do the boy now."

3. THE ÈLEGANTES

> **The langoliers had come.**
>
> **They had come for *him*.**
>
> **Craig Toomy began to scream.**
>
> **Stephen King, "The Langoliers."**

They call themselves the Èlegantes, fine city men, I think the translation is. They were fine at something long ago, but now have an altered state of thinking to go along with their munching of flesh—but strictly B-team, though. Unemployed soul-eaters, the rumor goes. Plus the Èlegantes are union. Now. They decided that since they were doing such a glorious job that they should at the very least get some recognition for it. Plus the people they ate were becoming low-class so under the new agreement those were debated upon first.

Then there was the recognition issue. And how do ya to get credit for a job well done, anyway? Complain to the public? No, so first the Èlegantes thought about suing for respect. But by the time "lawyers" became concrete things, what most people knew about lawyerin had become bad and suspicious. Next came just being nice about their work; not chomping everything with veracity. People did not appreciate this kindlier gentler approach.

Work slow-down and stoppages did it. None, not even the Four Horsemen would cross the strike line so everyone, including the suits were finally forced back to the table. The conditions were simple enough. The Èlegantes would only bid on special jobs. Either ones where delicateness was needed or complete eradication, like Atlantis or the genius who came up with the idea for shows like "Dog Eat Dog" or "Lost." The yeoman work, however, would fall onto the shoulders of the humans who were all too happy for such things. Everyone was delighted.

The Èlegantes decided to headquarter on the northeastern seaboard of what had become the US. Other conditions were that the humans would learn more from the Èlegantes and upon the death of the last fine city man, which would happen sometime after they had eaten their quota, there would be a massive display of eradication of people and their history; homage, you understand. Something to recognize the fact that Death's agents though having purpose, were still not the only professionals in the business.

One of the Èlegantes last jobs was eating this guy named Macky. The Èlegantes also secured deliveries of the *NY Times*, *Washington Post*, *Wall Street Journal*, and *Jane's Foreign Report*, newspapers and periodicals that would serve as progress reports to what the humans were doing just to make sure there was no overstepping of boundaries. You understand. The address was to local 1143 in New York City. They thought about a place called San Francisco but decided that was Ronald's place.

4. MACKY

This time Macky has finally, finally made it to the site. The site is a small patch of bluegrass. Surrounded by cement. But there are no combs, tonic water or special hair growth formula lying about. Nor does he hear, "Attend the tale of Sweeney Todd, his skin was pale and his eye was odd, he shaved the faces of gentleman, who never thereafter were heard of again," this time. When before, when he did hear those lines he had always stopped dreaming of finding the music box and chose to dream about anything else.

He thinks a woman sings those lines to him. A woman by the name of Glenda, who has settled into her new job as chauffer quite nicely. She should have sung to him before this point in his dream this time, but perhaps she will help him no more. Or was lazy since he was already at the patch.

Trees surround this patch of grass. In the middle of the patch was a rusted plate. He spate on his hands and pulled the plate up and threw it aside. He heard nothing. Macky was impressed that he had gotten this far. This was the same dream he has had for a while; coaxed on by a male voice, and discouraged by a female one, so this was the first time he actually went from standing on the cement to standing in the sanctuary.

The plate covered a not too deep hole. At about a foot down there was another steel handle. It was attached to a brown terra cotta pipe, yet it was pre-cut so as to expose its guts. It took two hands but Macky pulled this plate up and sat it aside.

A smell much like himself when he refused to wipe shook him and put him on his heels. He looked up at the sky and saw white, whiteness, the color of sketchbook pages.

When his body told him the smell was not okay but to step down anyway, he did.

In the pipe was a box. A music box. He reached down and plucked it out of the slow-moving water. The exterior of the box was metallic, mossy, and teal green in color. The box did not have a lock on it. He opened it, surprised to find out it really was a music box, though music did not play. It was lined with crushed purple velvet. He smiled. From under the velvet some small marbles jumped out and into the water. They fizzled and popped. He closed the box. He then crawled out of the hole holding the box next to his chest.

Really muddy, he opened the box again. There was still no music. That was okay; he did not need the box—the marbles were the important thing—but it sure was pretty. "So this was what I was so afraid of. Seeing marbles in sewer water. 'Hear me balls of steel and glass and glue! I, Mackaveilly, order you from the realm of dreams and the past and into the now! It is time for my quickening! Come now. Awake!'"

Macky giggled and put a hand over his big white buckteeth. Until the box flew open and those remaining marbles joined their brethren, sparkling and growing. Macky looked down. In their sparkle he saw his real future and ran. But it did not matter anymore. He had commanded them to come from one realm and into his, and the Èlegantes had.

5. BAD DANDY

"Never again."

The first time Bad Dandy heard those words he almost cried. Now leaning over the railing of the *Maria*, feeling the boot-knife, his only worldly possession, he understood, "Never again." He looks at his hands: fingers, fore and ring are six inches long. He has three-inch thumbs and pinkies. On a five-four frame. From shoulder to fingertip, he's thirty inches. His eyes always looked at your throat then straight down like he was wondering if you deserved the open slice move. But he was thinking of starting anew in America since that's what you did there. That's what the uppity boy told him you did there: he would miss the kid's fear though, however the kid had only one ticket and Bad Dandy had the only knife. Still, looking at that boy, all dandied up, gave O'Donnell inspiration for his new name.

Anyway, a secession and war were gonna breakout in the New World and Bad Dandy was gonna ply trade there. It was rumored the US appreciated a hard working paddy like himself. Someone who could keep those slaves down along with any highwaymen who had gotten out of control. Maybe a Hessian or Italian too, but Bad Dandy hadn't seen those races yet and wondered what they looked like. He was told that by the kid who was dressed as a petty aristocrat. Bad Dandy, also known as Little O'Donell you know, looking at the boy and smelling his perfume came up with being called Bad Dandy right then and there. Now he was expanding while keeping Lucky Time's admonition in his head. But the prospect of a job besides monkeying with Macky was very strong. Could both be done? Could the New World hold all that hope? He could dream, could he not? Oh the power of such things, but he would have to check himself.

        *   *   *

"I gotta make sure I'm on the right side, that's been my problem," Little O'Donell thought as the ship set sail en route to the United States. And patriarchy only listens to the market. "God sent the blight, but the British sent the famine," Bad Dandy, aka, Little O'Donell thought as he could not see his old land anymore. Muddy now, where it was once green. He use to be gay and not just psychopathic. Oh how he has changed. Different. How different?

Little O'Donell did not know. He only knew his adoptive parents were parceled off for being slow, plus their Lord's manor was burned down. Then running into Lucky Time and his proposal: If he wanted a higher position he would do well to leave, especially if he wanted to do this thing called retire. He never forgave his parents for being slow. And his father, for not being there to burn, loot, or kill the English and Irish "nobility," when it would have made him feel better inside.

Bad Dandy is not sixteen anymore. Some have even wondered if he ever really had what we would call parents.

When the *Maria* docked at Penn's Landing, Philadelphia, his contempt made him do a little cutting on himself. So much he was quarantined for what should have been long enough for the medical establishment to give him the once over. Twice even, and he had heard the rumors, knew that staying there meant he would die in some not so sterile cell infected with what they called typhus. And the worse of it was most of his fellow countrymen and women working in the hospital looked at those just off the boat as the problem.

As far as Bad Dandy was concerned, the only group that had some real transcendence were those in high government or business. Or at the very least those in the military. Then back to the idea of running a killing school. Yes, that way he could have some money and do a little stabbing around Philly, or even better, a place called Down South. That made Bad Dandy smile and remember the time Lucky Time had said Bad Dandy would be the next to be the prime mover if he did well enough.

Thinking of these roving opportunities after leaving the hospital and working odd jobs cheered Bad Dandy up. Enough that a fellow warder, Sean Riley, who had been looking his way for weeks, actually spoke to him. It was in the noontime chow line. "Let me tell you something boy-o, in whatever you do," and at this point the older gent looked around to make sure no one was listening, whispered, "do not become one of those niggers." He then erected himself, waiting to see his friend, the lunch counterer. When this older gent, Sean Riley, saw his friend he grinned and said "Hello Douglass. How is everything?" In Douglass' ear, "Between you and me, champ, I hope this is our last affair, eh?"

Douglass smiled. He had always liked Riley. Douglass, who was never a slave but most of his kin did not make it out of slavery said to Riley, "I do hope so. My wife frowns upon such rendezvous." They laughed and a supervisor gave Douglass the look that said enough fraternizing with the lower classes but both laughed a little longer. Bad Dandy almost smiled.

Riley came to love Douglass and his family, and not because Douglass helped Riley and O'Donell get cleared. Yes it was. Douglass and his wife Millie, both believers in the Gospel took both Riley and O'Donell in until they found places. O'Donell didn't need money for a new place though. He always had some. But since he kept her knives sharp, no one asked how he seemed to have more money and jewelry than any one else in the ghetto. Riley also got a job working under Douglass at the hospital, and both were promoted. But Riley was promoted over Douglass. Embarrassed, Riley gave a portion of what he thought was Douglass' money to him. That is how they got on.

One night Douglass and Riley died. Side by side. A Passer, that's a person who goes knocking on tenement doors, was looking for niggers to take Down South rapped on Riley's door. It seemed that the North was trying to rid itself of them, make them slaves. The cynics said that if the North had its way, they would sell them Down South then engage in hostilities saying that having slaves was an abomination. Cynics are right a lot of the time.

"I have been living here with mine for some time and have not seen as such," Riley said, "but it is eleven of the clock and you all should go elsewhere or run the risk of turning into such a creature." An argument ensued and Douglass came out to help.

"Why Riley, you liar; I see one at last! Right there! I think we should take you too, for being in co-hoots with such beasts. What would ever posses ya?"

Douglass, sensing his friend had gotten into some kind of trouble steeped in front of Riley.

"Don't you dare harm this man. He is a good and reverent man. And unlike the likes of this cabal is not prone to an inability to say no too strong drink. Go home and sleep off whatever fight is in your heads."

The Passer said, "And he talk pretty, too. He should bring us a nice prize."

A rope went around Douglass' neck and as he was being hauled away, Riley, his knife in his hands, cut the rope. Douglass fell and the Passer roped Riley, but Douglass came up with a few stones and was always a good one when it came to aim.

So they roped him again.

Their wives came out with knives, slashing horse and man but the posse still outnumbered them and drug the men away. Not to be sold but used as a lesson. So through the streets they went until the ropes went slack and the screaming stopped.

Bad Dandy saw all of this from the roof of their building. He was sharpening metal objects. He decided he would track the posse to their homes.

After the posse broke up for the night he crept into their tenement building with a hammer and handkerchief. The Passer first but to each room he went, first rousing the man by stuffing a monogrammed handkerchief down their throats then administered blunt knocks on the forehead. The first was always to make sure they were awake.

"I would not be doing this if you all had gotten down from your horses and engaged in a brawl and then took them. That would have been honorable. But on horse back?" And because Bad Dandy straddled each of them when he came to them they could not fight off the blows, nor scream louder than anyone to hear besides Bad Dandy. The walls heard though. And the bed sheets. Plus the straw used as a mattress and the floor. Soaked with blood. It was that night that Bad Dandy decided he would really be a great teacher and time was a wastin.

But a pre-Honest Abe's Army did not want Dandy. At first. Too eager at slapping and stabbing the recruits. So he was let go for a month and told to reapply as an instructor, which he did. But this time an old order, one in which he would teach individuals on the proper art of killing came to pass. These killers would work as an elite group and kill who they were told to kill. He liked the opportunity, having studied a little and knew big words. But their great big ideas on liberty confused him. So much he went to the shores of South Carolina to think it all over. He stood on the shore having drawn an outline of a classroom with his knife, leaving enough room to weave between the rows of desks. The sun was going down, stretching that glow back to the ancestors of all.

"Class, er, no one can control my desire, except me. Um, thinking about the ontology of power disturbs me, it always has, yet now there is the rumor of war. I have tried writing about it but such actions are emotional I hesitate to gather myself. Heed me, class, for I believe an ugly fight between the states is in the wind. Pondering this is over my head and drowning me. I have been called a pessimist, negative, told I live without hope or salvation. You will be told that too, later perhaps. Remember though that blood is the energy of power.

"But before delving into that there is also the worry that one might be looking too deeply for something. I don't . . . I'm no romantic. But I do lie about myself. Plus I do not believe a cigar can ever just be a cigar. It connotes a real ideal. Though so does the statement it rains on the just and unjust. But beneath power, if we look, is command. It is there. Either physical or no, power is having influence over another object. Yet for this power to be manifested there must be command. One has to command to truly be in power. I am trying to look at this problem from the bottom inside. Command is only the middle passage of action. The next level down is where it's at. Before getting there, I will say that we all want the heat of command. Not necessarily responsibility, but command. Not to lead, but power. We become daring when we leave the campfire for the bonfire. Can I get an amen?"

Bad Dandy stopped. It was night. It was high tide. The water surrounded him, rose above him. He bobbed up and down. He resumed his lecture.

"People, when you become the monsters of our profession, it will infect you. Hey! No passing notes during the lecture! Yes, it will get to you. That's why at night I can't sleep. Sweat trickles down my sides; my dreams still tell me I am on the outside. What will become of me? 'Candlesticks in the dark, visions of bodies being burnt, four walls just staring at a nigga, I'm paranoid, sleeping with my finga on the trigga . . .' And on the shore up there, a fortification up the shore from here, Fort Sumter's history will happen boys and girls. Will I, this time, get there in time? Why can't someone say to me, 'I finally looked to paint a picture of my whole life, and for me to end it would be so nice?' Because that would mean I died without even a blurb in the papers. A war is about start and I must get in it if I am going to finally make my mark.

"I am, you all are, gorillas, that yearn for the sweet nothings of knowing who I am; war's reward. Without it, all I can say is 'I hope you can't sleep and you dream about it, and when you dream I hope you can't sleep and you scream about it, I hope your conscience eats at you and you can't breath without it.'" What else to do? Is there another way to enlist you shitbirds? Will you all be my shining moments? Can Macky bring my glory to me? Will he, by his vainglory prove me worthy? Will he understand the game? Will he understand that any chance at Frenchie means doing the job to get the home?"

That was enough class.

Bad Dandy walked out of the water and into the area where the plantation houses rested. The night bugs made loud noises and that was good: Their songs masked the sound of feet, two groups of men, women, and children running past Bad Dandy to freedom. Black and white. Dandy smiled. He dug up a pair of machetes under a hanging tree. He had decided to freelance, so he's lying on his belly, on the outskirts of Giddy mansion, just until the last upstairs lights go off. He'll slip into Massa's house and cut Massa up then. And maybe Missus, if she's in cohoots.

There won't be much trouble getting in, either, since word has spread that a bad paddy was in the bush just waitin to hack on a rich Massa family. And if a house nigra gits in the way, he or she gits a whackin too.

6. BAD DANDY AND PUPIL

Bad Dandy has had a tough time keepin his slash and stab moves for practice dummies, but at least his classes have started. He is motivating his star pupil.

"The questions have always been the same, plebe. Always! And this one you always get wrong. Do you think this is funny?" Bad Dandy asks this of plebe cow Alice, aka Frenchie, who he is using the front-choke hold method on. "What are you trying to do Alice? Is Frenchie trying to P I S S me off? You got the answer to 'How's the cow?' but want me to believe that you do not know the definition of leather?" And her tanned skin, in the blue light that descends into this dungeon, shows her face as purple. He stops when he can no longer feel her pulse. Sighs. Gives her a handkerchief soaked with his sweat. She twitches and coughs. He is patient.

"Bad Dandy, freewoman cow Alice must inform you—"

"No no no, do not go on that way, you're starting to sound like that Ronald. The proper fraternity answer is, 'Sir, my cranium consisting of Vermont marble, volcanic lava, and African Ivory, covered with a thick layer of case hardened steel, forms an impenetrable barrier to all that seek to impress itself upon the ashen tissues of my brain. Hence, the effulgent and ostentatiously effervescent phrases just directed and reiterate for my comprehension have failed to penetrate and permeate the somniferous forces of my atrocious intelligence.'

"And for leather, the correct answer is, 'If the fresh skin of an animal, cleaned and divested of all hair, fat, and other extraneous matter, be immersed in a dilute solution of tannic acid, a chemical combination ensues; the gelatinous tissue of the skin is converted into a non-putrescible substance, impervious to and insoluble in water; this, sir, is leather.' That is all. They are tests of memory that double as markers of stages. The first stage is being in so much pain while being tested you dream of a life outside the lab. Two, I inhabit your dreams and tell you about the music box and the treasure inside it. You dream that and command the Èlegantes to come out and eat you. They do, making you anew. Then you are told to remember answers like 'How's the cow,' as you walk the streets, killing when you think you might be caught. When you recite that one, it is on to the next, which is the definition of leather. And if you do not know an answer you recite about the marble. You were so promising that I had decided to forgo you being eaten! And you were not thought of as special. Not like Macky.

"But Macky is farther back than you. He's so wishy-washy—won't answer to cow. Plus he ran away from the Èlegantes. Now he should have been eaten and spate back out right then and there but he ran. He's always running. Macky was supposedly to surpass me and I am to become a deity. Are you breathing okay? Sometimes I think someone else is trying to stop his training. He has not definitively opted out. I could love him if he would do that. Oh, what is to become of us, Frenchie?"

Bad carries her upstairs and into the medical hut. "You will rest here. Someone will take you back to the labs. Not for long though; I trust you will leave when you think you can remember the answers. All of them. For me it is back to monkey with Macky's program, ho hum, but I think I want be able to train more troops for the war. Gonna speed it up for him. Naw, no more troops, just Macky. And Frenchie. And anyone else I do please.

7. CRASHING CURIOUS GEORGE'S PLACE

Bad Dandy went to the house George lives in. Bad Dandy was not impressed. The man with the yellow hat's home wasn't as big as he had thought it would be. Especially with the furniture overturned. You could squeeze about fifty people into the living room, if they all agreed not to step on the broken clay and glass on the carpet. Or knock over piles of old magazines that double as drink and chip and dip stands. The fake skulls hanging from piano wire were safe enough, providing you are less than six-five. That really wasn't a worry to the big man though: he never invited anyone over six feet to his home.

The walls were red; the new color since Bad Dandy had come.

The hallway is still cluttered with fertility masks snarling at you, though. Teething at you. No one hangs out in the hallway anyway: it is only ten feet long. It connects the bathroom at one end and the living room at the other. The bedroom is off the left side if you were walking back to the john. In the master bedroom looking frightened is the man with the yellow hat, curled up and bleeding from having fought his way from the broken kitchen window through the living room to here. He's missing most of some of his fingers.

Bad Dandy sat at the foot of the bed, the man at the head. Bad Dandy tried to be cordial, not wanting the man to be completely fingerless. This way he might still be invited to cool reindeer game parties and Easter egghunts when all this was done and forgiven. Bad Dandy took a long drag from a cigarette then spoke.

"You know you have a quaint place here, you really do. I would like to be invited back after things have . . . happened. I like the new color on the walls, don't you? Red is such a festive color, it really is. Makes you want to have friends over, right? Fer Xmas? After you get fixed up and therapied, of course."

Puff puff Bad Dandy puffed away. The smoke was blue-gray. In the dim room all you could see was the shape of Bad Dandy and the lit end of his cigarette inside that blue-gray cloud. Bad Dandy flicked ashes on the comforter; disappointed they did not catch. He asked the question. "Where is he, man with the yellow hat? Where is Curious George?"

The man shook. His trembling reminded Bad Dandy of little children yet the moon showed the man with the yellow hat as old, lean, lanky, slashed, and holding some charm in his good hand while the other was a mess in his mouth. If he spoke blood would run from his thumb and middle finger and pinky down his elbow unto the bed making a dark pool, so he kept it in his mouth.

"Foff foo odd andy."

A longer drag then out. Dandy believed he could have been a pretty decent decadent lounge singer, white wearing stacks, black zoot suit pants, and a white opened, buttoned, fake, silk shirt with a sweat drenched hanky. He would even have a few Zodiac necklaces dangling from his hairy chest. He's not hairy but that can be fixed. And a spray bottle of fake sweat. Because he is all performer. But the blade and bone. How could anyone not answer when Lucky Time called to tell you your future?

"Man with the yellow hat, I don't mind whacking on you some more if I have to, but c'mon, you know how it is; George has to got to go into the stew pot.

That is his part in all this. Let's not make it anymore than that please." Bad Dandy showed his machete again. "I'm trying to help you, man with the yellow hat. I've even called the authorities. But if I'm here with all this shit on your wall, they'll think that you went native. If I leave before they arrive it was a crazy burglary. It's the difference between shots, treatment, cages, and spending Xmas making little make-believe snow angels instead of having me over. That and I know you probably make dynamite eggnog. Have you ever karaoked?"

"Foff foo?" The man shook his charm at Dandy. "Uff foo! Fuump foo Fump foo odd andy!"

Bad Dandy grabbed an ankle with one hand then down came the other hand with the machete in it. White feathers flew up and floated back down. Blood coughed out from this

new wound as the man swallowed more fists of blood, shook his charm and cried. Bad Dandy remembered that he was going to stick to fingers.

"Oh. I said I was only going to cut off fingers, huh? Anyway, you bore me man with the yellow hat. But you seem to want to fight me to the end. Okay, but I don't know what you see in him," Bad Dandy stepped off the bed, putting the super tool back into his box, "but before I take out his guts and heart I'll ask him if the feeling is mutual. It's my guess he's using you. You know how monkeys are. Don't be fooled, he might have a following, but some of those picture frames are not flattering." Bad Dandy walked over to the charm and bit its head off.

The authorities arrived soon after, asked some questions, got little help, dusted for prints, and flipped a coin. Tails. This was a botched burglary plus assault.

Dandy laughed as he swung through the trees.

CHAPTER TWO

Blow the horn, play the fife, beats the drum, so, slowly.

Glory **soundtrack**

1. BUSTIN LOOSE

Macky has a glasshouse. This house is on one side of the third floor. It takes up about a third of the laboratory. It is on the left. It is twenty by twenty. When the door forms, it faces out to the open part of the lab. Macky's glasshouse has a lavatory, sink, and gurney. Plus a few humanizing items: pens, a pair of clothes, and sketchbooks.

Awake not wanting to dream about the Èlegantes dream again, Macky decided to think about writing. He was alone. The glass that enclosed him would not rotate for a little while, bringing a labcoater or two with some of those pills.

The cage, that is what Macky calls it, is comprised of rotating glass panels, vertical louvers, to be precise. The panels turn periodically, letting in the bright rays of the sun. Plus, because it is made of glass it gets humid, making him grateful for the water the labcoaters give him and the soft breezes from Mother Nature. Especially when the women labcoaters come in. He smells their perfumes and anticipations. He has had dreams where he does to them what they have done onto him.

At certain times of the day the louvers turned clock-wise from their position of side to side to about six o'clock. When that happens the four panels in the center of the cage that face the open part of the lab swell to five times their original size pushing the rest closer to together, so you can get an arm through. Then those four turn horizontal again. If you have a magnetic card and swipe it on either side of the panels that make this door you can open it. That is why the glass only turns in the daytime when there are always a few labcoaters on hand.

Diary entry

Dear Diary, today I made up my mind! I'm going to escape. I'm not letting that dreadful dream keep me here. Plus, there's Frenchie. I still want her. I want to touch her. I want to devalue her by running her name through the mud. To make her live in shame with me. I love her. I want to destroy her, diary, to make her ashamed, broken. I want to sex her up and shout my name when I do it.

Bad Dandy told me all that is possible if I have purpose. The idea of purpose has perked up my handwriting too, see? Look at how lovely I write! I could get a job writing wedding invitations! But my training has barely started. I want her and he will help but when Bad Dandy smiles there is always blood on his lips and meat in his teeth. No matter. I have a card to sweep, no, swipe I mean—the type they use to enter and exit my cage. Plus I've seen where to go whom to see. I think it's a he. His name is Bad Dandy. Did I say that already?

2. THIS IS HELP?

The gods have smiled on Macky. The two main labcoaters began arguing and shoving again. Over the same issue but this time it all came out.

You'd think the argument would be over the fact that their test subjects keep disappearing and sometimes, re-appear, but no. Something more emotional.

"Okay Gordan, we've gone around and around without actually saying it but no more. Since your celebration vacation there's been a problem around here. Personally, I wouldn't accept an award for a fast-acting non-acme forming face foundation and a better penis pump—.and what self-respecting man needs one? I mean supplement s are one thing, but then you've also allowed her to come between our work and us. This lab cannot continue getting funding with such shoddy ethics. Plus it's your fault we have this type of dissension amongst the ranks anyway."

The ethics Jimmy H. is talking about have nothing to do with nuclear energy or high altitude warfare. Unless you could harness the high power of love.

"Jimmy, I, and not you bought a mail-order bride from Russia! There!

That's where she's from and if I want her to strut those got damn long legs up and down the halls of this place that's my business! Don't hate the player, hate the sport, eh?"

"But she's screwing the entire staff you idiot."

Quiet. The three women on the team leaked that, all at different times, all to Jimmy. At all those times they had to lean over a table when the only other one in the room was Jimmy. All in that outraged hurt voice. Plus the low-cut blouses with the push up and miracle bras. Pouty lips. This was war and they needed a man to protect their honor. Plus if anyone should lose his or her job by being a sex-whistle blower, it should be Jimmy-the liplicker when you walk by-Hawthorne.

"You lie, Jim."

"No I don't Gordan, and I have the pictures and names and two videos and a sound project to prove it."

"You're whoring my wife? Cuckolding your noted superior and winner of the Copper Glob award, Jim? I could have your job, beat-off boy."

"I wouldn't put up with that shit," someone yelled and pushed Jimmy into Gordon while others yelled "kick his ass" and "I'd smash his ugly face in with a Bunsen burner."

The third time around it was Jimmy by himself who pushed Gordon who reciprocated. Slapping next. And what no one saw was him sneak in and monkey with some of the toxic vials. He was wearing coveralls with wrenches, screwdrivers and a set of schematics for the ventilation system in his back pocket. Macky did not see Bad Dandy come in or out, either. Macky had his back to them, thinking about writing a novel. Bad Dandy walked out with a smile on his face but he wished he had something sharp and now bloodied from being into somebody's guts.

Gordon grabbed a vial of liquid floating in oil and threw it at Jimmy. It went wide and shattered along the back wall as white and black fumes rose from the spill and filled the room. A hand tossed five more vials into the lab then shut the door. One of the females hit the red button and speakers from the ventilator system yelled BUZZ! BUZZ RRING from the ceiling. The floor rattled. WARNING, FIRE, WARNING, FIRE. The labcoaters swung their arms and hands back and forth, looking for colleagues. This was how they had practiced it. In the event of an emergency they would gather to hold hands then walk out in a single file line. They could have done that this time too if their hands were not blistering milky, and their skin sloughing off. Their lungs too waterlogged to convert anything to anything, too. They died there. Five labcoaters. Hand in hand.

It took the system an hour to figure out that the fumes were bad, turn off the vent system, and then suck any remaining bad air into a safety sealed anteroom. The time in the OSHA manual stipulated was ten minutes. Macky saw and heard the labcoaters cry and beg for breath but he knew he would survive. His house had its own vent system. That and the glass would turn at 3:30. This emergency began at 2:00. So, as the glass panels turned sideways at 3:30, Macky only faintly smelled the dead air. He pulled the card out from under his sleep roll and swiped.

He would have stayed if they had asked. It was a home, you know. Plus he had obtained most of their language and could write. All they had to do was explain the dreams to him. He was already their destiny or at least their means to one. But he also believed there might be more than that for him somewhere. He was of average weight and weight, five-ten, hundred and ninety pounds, and could look like almost anyone. He only ballooned when they forced those pills down his throat.

Macky knows something about fashion. He prefers to wear tweed jackets with elbow patches, beige button down shirts, tweed ties, pennies in his penny-loafers, white socks and red pants, so those were the same items he zipped into an overnight bag. Also tinted safety goggles.

Having stuffed a few pens and a chapbook into his inside right jacket pocket he leaped out of the cage. He then ran over to the fridge, took some food and got to the door. It was not locked. The hall, short of the sounds of sirens and motherly warnings about leaving orderly, was empty. He walked out. He wandered about how easy this was. So what? Macky was now free.

He had found freedom and wanted to know about Bad Dandy and that way. Plus the dreams and the other destiny: job, home, Frenchie.

*   *   *

The world was a lot different from when Macky last saw it. He thought that as he tripped over broken concrete. Once, and for a long while this was a fine sidewalk, complete with wheelchair ramps. Now chunks of trip-up concrete preyed on unsuspecting walkers. His eyes spied a dusty bottle top lying on the lawn that use to be green. Now dirt and broken seed rested atop the cracked earth. The bottle top had writing in it. "Teams of juice guys travel across the USA in Nantucket Nectar Winnebagos towing bottle-shaped trailers filled with Nectars." The last time he was out nectars were young cute girls but you can't get a girl in a bottle. Not if she were fully developed anyway. Unless you blew her up. And if that was the case why just women? Or men? What about a family dog? It did not matter. Nor did looking up at the building that was home. It too looked dry. Some labcoaters were laying face down twitching. Sirens were coming and other labcoaters were bleeding from the mouth, tearing at their eyes and pulling dead skin off their bodies. He started to cough. So he left.

A little out of sight, Èlegantes had heard him cough.

In a tree still watching all of this wearing a protective mask was Bad Dandy. Bad Dandy had told the reconnoitering Èlegantes that Macky was going to escape.

*   *   *

Free now, nothing to do except walk, which he did. Macky walked until he saw something that was all truth: a strip mall. And a house of worship and smoothies to boot. This was Macky decided a little spiritual guidance would help.

A cat strolled up to Macky while he prayed. The kitty bugged him. It was all white and wet and large. Looked like a leopard. It was a sunny but raining day. The statue he was praying to was also outside but it had a cover. The mat for kneeling was soggy though. This temple was a health store and fitness vendor. There was no one out here at the far end of Stoner's Mall. This was his place of worship for the time being. The stores were closed. Plus he had no money.

*   *   *

Oh to Christ was there another way? But this cat wanted to sit on his loafers, which were attached to his ankles, attached to his legs to his hips and up to his head. Macky was not much bigger than the piece of fur.

*   *   *

There were noses and mouths in the distance, sniffing and puffing. Macky had thick slivers of grade A concrete in all his pockets. There was still too much daylight to use them, though. Cars rolled by behind him; alarms in all of them. How useful are those things? Women are taught to say fire instead of rape.

*   *   *

The fur finally stopped wanting his feet and stood on its hind legs to try to rest its head on Macky's. Was it trying to get him to touch it? Or push him off the mat? He smiled thinking that this cat would never give up. To give it a reward Macky took a step from the mat and on to the sidewalk. He raised one of the slivers of concrete out of his back pocket. Do it, no. Do it. Come on Macky, show some stomach. Damn, if victory wasn't so gosh darn short.

*   *   *

Macky smelled cigarette smoke. It encapsulated a being he thought he knew. It puffed disappointed smoke rings. Bad Dandy walked towards Macky, the smoke hiding his body.

"How's the cow, chickenshit?"

Macky jumped back at the sight of someone wrapped in smoke, wearing a cloak, walking from between the GNC and Nordic Trac stores. He could not see a face or make out the body. Macky backed up some more and looked around for witnesses, just in case.

"I didn't do what you thought I should have."

The smoking cloak closed the distance.

"No, cow. The answer is, 'Sir, she walks, she talks, she's full of chalk. The lactile fluid from the female of the bovine species is highly prolific to the nth degree, sir!' Okay?" Macky stepped into the street. Fluorescent orange gums then red-wined teeth appeared behind a cloak still lost in smoke.

"I am who you seek, bovine, but I must be quick on these matters for there are other things I must do. There is a place in history for you but that is enough for you on that matter, for now. Macky, you have to be eaten right away. And take the lessons from the train if you want to meet Frenchie. But you must do the transformation then get that new career, then the home, and then you get the girl.

"You can do all of this. You think of yourself as low and despised by the labcoaters not to mention people in general. Can't blame them for their feelings, yet I know you were cast out and into the world of experimentation. You were poured out like water, were you not? Your strength has dried up and dogs bite at your heels. Or cats. But you fight back, right? Yet you are reduced to this. Here you are, having escaped and still not amounting to anything. Plus not squashing the cat just now. You. . . have potential still, but you will have to follow me completely, yes? Follow me, mad cow disease."

Macky tried to put it all together on an empty stomach. He could use a sandwich or at least a hibachi, pigeons, and some charcoal briquettes. The food from the lab was eaten seven days ago. He had managed to make a week's worth of trail mix, washing it down with rain water, but that also was gone. Once he heard about something called Ramadan and almost cried at how some suffer to be reborn and rejuvenated and made again. He would rather have a body and mesquite. Is this what monkeys and cows ate? It was going to take the whole journey to understand this so he settled for a question.

"Who are you?"

Sleep started to take Macky. His knees buckled and he staggered toward the mat. He lay there then crawled into the fetal position. Right before he fell asleep he he heard the cloaked figure say, "I am Bad Dandy."

*   *   *

When Macky woke the stars were losing their solid grip on darkness, letting small portions of lighted morning take the sky. He looked at his clothes and decided he needed a place to stay while contemplating. That and with all the rumors of Southern secession going on, getting off the street would not be a bad idea. There was also the residue from the world of labcoaters and sterile things that had forced certain opinions on him that he wanted to exercise. Then Bad Dandy, but this time the shepherd would have to wait. He was outside now, looking for some good Sam, a Good Samaritan to help him forget his powerlessness.

Time to go house shopping.

Tap pity

tap pity

tap pity

tap, slide.

Turn. Tap

pity tap

pity tap

pity tap

pity, slide,

turn. Tap

pity tap

pity tap

pity tap

slide, turn.

Tap pity

tap pity

tap pity

tap, slide,

nothin. Go to the next corner.

      The strolling was taking up large parts of the day and Macky started

to believe he heard munchings when finally, from the inside his car, a good

Sam smiled. Macky smiled back. This one looked like he was going to help.

Macky had every intention of paying such generosity back in a way that

would go a long way in reconciling not being able to say no to the labcoaters.

Just like magic Macky was in the car looking at Sam's wedding band while they were in front of the Good Sam's house. But no, damn if this Sam's house didn't look like a dump. Even from the outside. Macky whacked this Sam on the forehead with a sliver a few dozen times, pushed this Good Sam out of the car and drove off, resuming looking, thinking to himself again.

*　　　*　　　*

Macky's a pleasing monkey.

*　　　*　　　*

He didn't want to be an experiment anymore, so the sugar was the next step. He damaged his teeth just like a friend said. One tooth way back in the back of his head. A wisdom tooth, bottom right. Stubborn cur. When Macky was younger there was surgery to leave him with forty teeth but that one wouldn't budge. He took it as a sign. As long as that one was strong and healthy nothing would change. Yeah, that molar was his magic center honey pot for change. If he could make it go bad, Tooth would throb, a signal to the one who would change him. That came to Macky during a lab test while he was suffering from being fed feeding and thought why me oh why? And a voice told him that he could live believing that it rained on the just and the unjust, or engage the enemy with complete bayonet assault strikes to the head, making their life short. And meet Frenchie.

CHAPTER THREE

I am an angel, stands in the corner, nobody sees me

Living Colour

1. THE LIFE IS LONG

Bad Dandy, on his life:
The life is too long.The life is too long.The life is too long.The life is too long.
The life is too long.The life is too long.The life is too long.The life is too long.
The life is too long.The life is too long.The life is too long.The life is too long. The life is too long.The life
is too long.The life is too long.The
life is too long.
The life is too long.The life is too long.The life is too long.The life is too long.
The life is too long.The life is too long.The life is too long.The life is too long.
The life is too long.The life is too long.The life is too long.The life is too long. The life is too long.The life
is too long.The life is too long.The life is too long..
The life is too long.The life is too long.The life is too long.The life is too long.
The life is too long.The life is too long.The life is too long.The life is too long.
The life is too long.The life is too long.The life is too long.The life is too long. The life is too long.The life
is too long.The life is too long.The life is too long.
The life is too long.The life is too long.The life is too long.The life is too long.
The life is too long.The life is too long.The life is too long.The life is too long.
The life is too long.The life is too long.The life is too long.The life is too long. The life is too long.The life
is too long.The life is too long.The life is too long.
The life is too long.The life is too long.The life is too long.The life is too long. The life is too long.The life
is too long.The life is too long.The life is too long
But failure, is not success.

2. WINDOW SHOPPING

Macky ran the car into a tree to see the windshield shatter. If he got the opportunity, game on. For now it's back to the walk. The residences all looked unfriendly: suicidal grass and wilted trees flipped him off. The sidewalks sounded hollow. It sounded like there was a good inch of concrete under his feet, if that. After that, loose sand. When he thought about it he sped up. In the music dream the way was revealed: the eaters of matter, the Èlegantes. They and the flesh hackers made the world anew. Macky felt that Bad Dandy was one of the flesh hackers. He wondered, almost, if Bad Dandy would really take him to Frenchie. Or at least get him some food. He's fasting like he's supposed. Plus, if he came into sight of food he'd throw it away, but a bologna and cheese would hit the spot about now.

Ah, a neighborhood with an unvandalized neighborhood watch sign. This was a soft street. Yards a-plenty with dandelions, daffodils and plastic duckys aligning the driveway. Small green lawns hedged a good two or three inches into the soil, showing you the viscerality of agricultural husbandry. Yellow smiling faces plus the faded "baby on board" stickers on the Volvos. Rainbow signs on the BMWs. Nice looking apartment houses next to nice homes, that mixed neighborhood stuff that the labcoaters hated.

Another Good Sam came running towards Macky because he had begun limping and moaning. His A-game, workin it. Macky smiled in that way you assume he's thinking, "Oh brother, do you think you can you spare a dime?"

Diary entry

Dear diary, yesterday I had tubes in my mouth all the way down to my tummy. That made me remember the day I heard that Econo-Mac-Lab was supposed to be safe for me. That made me think of my childhood.

I had always been good at being a mascot or pet. Have to be with children around for they might hurt you. I was a happy youngster, but I was never one of them. I knew that.

I remember sitting on the back porch, sweating to the oldies in 110 heat, that means more than 35 degrees Celsius, you know, watching other children light fire crackers that would go pop when the gunpowder finally ignited. When they finished with the firecrackers they looked at each other. The smallest of the group ran away with the rest laughing and giving chase with lighters in their hands while flies and mosquitoes fondled me. My drink had separated into ice on the top, melted ice below, a layer of alcohol, then the sugar. That was living. But the sun went down.

Back then me and tooth and body were mostly one, the way children and their bodies are one. I cottoned many compliments about my teeth. Then the event that made my life unsafe and lab living safer.

It was recess and it was lunchtime. Outside it was bully-time. But it wasn't pick on the kid with glasses day. Or pick on the smart kid day. Instead it was pick on the chubby kid day. And they did. I wonder where the theys live. Under rocks? Down by a trash dump? No, I think the dump is too nice a place for the theys. The theys must live under the rocks you see drenched by the men with vomiting eyes who sleep on busy streets.

The chubby kid was Raymond Reynolds, the third. He wasn't just chubby he was chubby and dumb. And was really the 1st anyway. If he had been a computer whiz he could have hid in that group for it wasn't the computer geek's time. Plus those geeks had their own group, an advantage, for bully groups don't normally attack whole groups.

We all had recess at the school's playground. The yard had four sets of red swings, two pink roundabouts, a couple of benches made from real redwoods, a metal sliding-board, and a sandbox. They circled Ray Rey in the sandbox. He made a break for it but chubby kids aren't very fast. They dragged him to the swings. Put him on one and started to push him higher and higher. If he jumped before they said to he was gonna get knuckles and Nikes in his mouth for a week. Those on the roundabouts stopped spinning.

Where were the teachers, our protectors? Didn't we pay taxes for protection? That's what the evening news guy called it: protection money. But he was talking about the police. When I was taken, I wasn't paying taxes.

When Ray Rey was too high and could go no higher they hollered "Jump!" For a second it was like he was levitating. I wish I had a camera. Then he started moving again. Forward but on his back. A few jumped off the benches and ran away. Then his feet came down rotating his body forward as he moved through the air tumbling with the greatest of ease! Our protection came out. Someone must have tipped them off, just like on the show "Crimestoppers."

Ray Rey came down doing mid air forward rolls once, twice, his face leading as his forehead first WHAM! on the end of the sliding board. It reverberated a funny Wooming noise and I laughed. Ray Rey didn't see the humor. He yelled and screamed. Then he cried. Some of the other kids cried too. He had raised the bar for being messed up by the bullies so everyone else knew that their fate would be worse still.

Ray's head began to grow then a knot formed started to swell n stuff and I was told he wet himself. The protection was pretty steamed and came down on the bullies. Then everyone else. Anyway, the bullies decided to call off picking on the rest of us for a whole month. It was called their cooling off period. I took the time to get really skinny even though I was being given to the labcoaters. I was gonna be safer with science my parents cooed. I'm not sure, but that was the first time I felt a tooth throb because I surrounded it with confection sugar. The tingle gave me the sense that I must be made for something else, something better.

The labcoaters fed Macky pills that made him not want to stop eating. He even tried to eat the bars on his cage. Twice. All the while tears fell for he was trying to not eat. But Macky did become a prized science winner. Twice. But the Golden Glob only went for the more important discoveries.

3. THROWN AWAY

The new Good Sam had to spare more than a dime. He had to have patience too for Macky threw plastic bags of squid away. Away the oily fig leaves that had meat in them. Meat. The Neapolitan ice cream, the feta, oh wait, cop a feel, then thrown away. The lean seasoned smoked turkey, chronic flavor from farmers who fed their turkeys the good wholesome before taking their lives . . . all. Why? All that because Bad Dandy said so. Let it be written, so let it be done.

Bad Dandy wants to dip his foot in the blood of his enemies.

Bad Dandy does not like Macky.

Macky does not fully understand the Èlegantes.

4. NIGHTMARE

Macky's depression via hunger kept him sleepy. The new Good Sam wanted to talk a little but Macky would always drift off. The only time Macky stayed awake was when Sam's friend came over.

Macky is drifting off now, back to the barber. He appears in a barbershop but runs out when he sees heads on the floor. The sidewalk he stands on evolves into a field of sprouting daffodils. Singing. The yellow in the middle of the yellow petals make him think of his parents. The daffodils are his family, he is finally reunited and not just with mom and dad, but grandmama and grandpappa, ancestors all the way back to Lillith.

Glende's singing falls as the sound of marching rises. Macky sees the daffodils wilt as the marching gets stronger. Gunfire. Cannon fire. And gray-white smoke of powder falls from the sky. A fife and drum corps limp in unison across a far away hill. As the flowers now fall down wounded their stalks spurt blood at him to the beat of left right left right left right march. Glende whispers, "What is prettier Macky, the marching or the flowers? The marching, or the flowers? Macky, which is prettier?"

Too late.

CHAPTER FOUR

Pressure pushing me down

Queen

It's gettin' harder to cope; sometimes I feel like I'm the one doing dope

geto boyz

Diary entry

Dear Diary, I'm whining again. Plus I'm down and mostly out. The Good Sam and me are getting along fine; though no we're not, so it's got to be me. Had a dream last night but didn't answer its question. I'm broken but going forward. There, I said it. That was the first time I said it since I left. Even now I can only write it.

I wonder what types of chemicals were in the air at the lab. I think Bad Dandy made the air go bad. I have talked long enough. It is time to go jerk that chicken.

1. THE RELAX REWARD

theohmsoundtheohmsoundtheohmsoundtheohmsoundtheohmsoundtheoh

msound

the jerk begins   **his tooth throbs the ohm sound**

oh so the tooth doth pound His blood runs out his head

making tooth get more from less

using less for more Painslam

is in   **his tooth is throbbing the ohm**

sound

Macky's mouth now The tooth tells painslam to go from the

bottom last molar on the right to the top black canine hanging from the

bleeding gum Across the bridge to the left side behind his ear up to the left

temple hurry back down across to the nose then up to the

forehead trip back down his top lip down the whole right side of his face to

both arms to   **his tooth throbbed the ohm**

sound

fingers and thump thump thump ring ringing

someone's at

the door he comes in

theohmsoundtheohmsoundtheohmsoundtheohmsoundtheohmsoundtheoh

msound

2. EASY ACCESS

Bad Dandy doesn't have a key. Bad Dandy doesn't have a driver's license. Bad Dandy doesn't have an age anymore. His dogtag says, "Made in the USA." He walks the streets looking for action and helps special people transcend. Kind of. He heard Macky's pain.

3. EVEN MORE EASY ACCESS

Dandy sleeps in refrigerators in junkyards all over the world. Lucky Time runs the future. Lucky Time picked Bad Dandy to succeed him. But Bad Dandy has tests to pass and Macky is the hardest.

In this junkyard Bad Dandy has a little metal shed.

Bad Dandy sometimes carries a staff. It has been rumored that he can part things down the middle.

In the shed there are fluorescent lights attached to the ceiling. The shed is eight by eight. No windows. He keeps a little wardrobe here, for performances; another career, something even for after retirement. That of being a seamstress for a performer: himself. There are plastic models of women's torsos in here. Different sizes. Of men too. And children. Fibers and threads and sharp leather cutting scissors and scalpels. He keeps a little jerk chicken here for snackin. He does not starve. His teeth are fine.

He kills in different parts of the world to rid himself of depression. On ships and small boats too. Sometimes he hitches rides and kills the drivers. Then, if the driver has a family Bad Dandy drives there and kills them too— but only to keep sharp for teaching others. Killing doth come easy to Dandy.

It helps him keep an even tilt on life since he bores easily so he's a liberal. He likes to wrap himself in shrouds made of Chinese silk and Egyptian cotton and at night you see just this white shroud and orange eyes. Or maybe midnight-black. For Bad Dandy you must look and dress the part. No need to take vows of hunger or poverty, which is for the foolish. He will catch Curious George.

He has entered this Good Sam's house to tell Macky, "finished or not, that is enough. Tomorrow go to Le Shack."

Macky stopped, having not been able to bring out much anyway but oh the effort. He is happy to have heard the door to the bedroom open, those words, and then the front door slam shut.

Diary entry

Dear diary, Bad Dandy has a heavy toolbox. There's string in it. Needles and thread, strong sewing needles, scalpels, crystals, stuffing, scissors, different colored fabric cotton and a pretty assortment of velour remnants. Plus a machete. He looks at me in the same way he would if it were in his hand, I think.

Sometimes, at night, I worry he will want to visit it on me.

                    *   *   *

 The next night outside "Le Shack of Many Poots," Dandy spied Macky throwing a punch at the waiter.

        Macky had said his cut of lamb had chips of bone in the meat, which when he chomped down, cracked the wrong tooth. That was too much in a place with the fake real moss trees with Spanish kudzu that had genuine flies on them. They looked liked horse flies but did not seem to want to bite flesh. The shiny black flies just seemed to want to stick to the pale greenish trees with dusty leaves. But Macky is partial to his teeth.

        So the waiter who did not warn him about this hazard deserved a strike to the gut.

The waiter knew Aikido. Macky and his energy rolled into the street. He then rolled away from an oncoming city bus but was still struck by the back bumper. Pain slammed the tooth. When he stood he saw a body in a cloak throw a hamburger at him. Bad Dandy was across the street. No one else was there to scoop it up. Bad Dandy had a whole bag of them. Bad Dandy threw another one, this time Macky caught it in his teeth. Macky then gobbled up the one on the ground.

He knew Bad Dandy would be here for him if he followed most of his instructions. Eating less was the main point. To the point where his body would eat itself. Macky walked across the street. Bad Dandy walked into the alley. Macky followed. Bad Dandy stopped when he couldn't hear pieces of traffic anymore.

Bad Dandy with his white teeth, orange, turning to red gumline, woolly salt and pepper hair dropped the bag of burgers at Macky's feet. He stood four inches from Macky.

"I will call you Elsie and not Macky, for you are still a cow, do you hear me? How's the cow, Elsie?"

"Yeah, I mean yes, and thank you. I'm—"

"Wrong wrong wrong you answer all the way wrong!"

"Hungry?"

"Wrong wrong wrong you answer all the way wrong! It is filled with chalk! And the lactic acid in your bovine mouth is right at home Elsie, yes? Keeping the teeth strong? Well, stomp on your family then."

"But I'm hungry and no one else is here. What about I deny in the morning? I'll start over then?"

"No, dumb cow. Learn from me. Transform the Elsie in you. Let the Èlegantes do you. Or do you want to be served between slices of wheat bread for the labcoaters? Will yourself to escape from your past cow. You've done some of it, you forced your tooth's acceptance."

"That was easy."

"Oh shut up, grass muncher. Bad Tooth would have been happy being a good tooth in a pile of teeth thrown away behind any dentist's office. You saw differently. No ordinary Elsie could have done that. Finish what you have started."

Bad Dandy looked over Macky's shoulder to see people looking at them.

"Think of it from the standpoint of Frenchie as well. She would be greatly impressed knowing you could stomp your denial. I could tell her and you could meet her for dancing. Oh yes, I can see it now, the Frenchie sitting at a table listening to some pretty boy spinning, or even better, DJ Ricky, yet waiting for some real Mr. Goodbar to come by. Romantic, yes? Ricky is good for the solid beats but this is desire. Let's set it all up"

As Bad Dandy stood still, silent, a guitar was strummed, then a ba-badom, ba-badom, ba-badom, ba-badom four repeater groove began. The writer of "Honky Tonk Woman" would be proud. A little high Hawaiian twang sounds off riff and there was grass under their feet. Underbrush on the left and right.

Bad Dandy started to move his lower body in place, left arm up as if he were going to take a pledge, the other clasping the right shoulder blade of Macky.

"Cow, do you hear that?"

"What?"

Bad Dandy frowned. "Listen. Monkey see, cow do. Now, put your left arm up as if you were about to be sworn in."

Macky did.

"Good, cud. Now the other arm on top of mine."

"Sir—"

Bad Dandy grabbed his throat with one hand while the other clutched his nuts, squeezing and turning both. "Oh hoof n mouth disease," the underbrush, grass began to wilt, "do not ever interrupt a dance lesson." Bad Dandy let go. Macky staggered back but Bad Dandy had his shoulders and shook him erect. Bad Dandy smiled at the fear in Macky's eyes. The underbrush, grass and tropical trees started to show up again, in this ally.

"Okay moo, we'll try and approach it from a different angle.

"The techno-trance beat is back going bump bump bump, bump hump hump hump, hump hump, bump. The people are diggin it, true. Couples dancing, some with that 'Christ why did I agree to dance' look in them. It's cool though. Some are doing their Charlie Brown Xmas dance in close proximity to a warm body. Then there are the girls in a group dancing, celebrating grrrl power. But so what? None of these are Frenchie!"

And that was true. Yet something else flashed in his mind and rested there. On the creep creepy tip though, for if Bad Dandy knew what Macky was thinking he would have been mad. What flashed in Macky's mind was:

If you wanna

ride, then ride the white horse. If you wanna ride,

then ride the white horse. Boom, boom boom boom boom,

boom, boom boom boom, as the house beat syncopated the

feelings of rightness, that he was safe, loved. That

he was strong, that he had a fan. The girl, cloned,

from Osaka, was along the walls, wearing

high high heels, keeping them all at five-four, two foot long jet-black hair, or

two-inch

cropped short black, black hair, black mini, black

leather vest with zippers, barely holding all together.

Their eyes, half open, and brown tear-droplets, burned onto the right side of

their face, every other half inch, going to the chin, the underside of it, neck,

down to the right breast. Lips pouty, ready to be kissed. Chokers around their

necks, pulling them, tattooed numbers on their left wrists. Neon red lipstick,

hmm, *If you wanna*

ride, then ride the white horse, yeah, why not. He

rolled up a dollar bill, put part of it in his left

nostril, *white*, *horse*, and laid the open end on the

table. He looked up, they were all just looking at

him, him, and no one else. And no one else was at the

table either, just him, and a mound of dreams. He had

left his loyalty and duty at the door. It was too

hard, too little gratitude, to continue. He snorted up

and and and *If you wanna ride*, nothing. Nothing.

Again. The booze, crank, now this mound of dreams, but

nothing. A tear crawls down the right side of his check, chin, and underside,

of his neck, down to the right breast. It left a

silver streak, flashing with the strobe, and if you

looked at him, *horse*, you could see the tear

splitting his face, opening the neck, exposing

another, darker layer of skin. The girls just bounced

away, their asses brushing against the wall, their chests

arched at him.

And he stirred in the middle of a Greyhound bus terminal, against

the wall a few feet from the women's bathroom. He made his

way into the male's then looked at his face. The

silver streak was gone, but a faint scar remained. Stay on the

rampage or leave it and glory alone.

He remembered the sweaty smells of the girl and the

music started to come back into his head. *Horse.* He felt his

clothes-not the old rags he was now wearing but the black

leather trenchcoat, the satin baggie pants, the tailored shirt, how

those things felt. The sunglasses. He felt his mouth

and the teeth that he exposed to scare little kids. He

still had the tooth.

In the mirror, his friend, the answer once again

came into focus. "Emma. I will go to her, and she will

help me. We love each other."

If you wanna ride, then ride the white horse.

A blinking disco floor! You see her from across this crowded hole in the wall. You are drunk and hungry. Your belly is converting the calories from the beer and gin to keep you going. Frenchie, you, her, she sees you out of the corner of an eye and puts on glowing heroin brown lipstick. You get to her table and the rest of the club fades away. No house techno DJ here. Grrl power, the drunk guys who just lean against the wall wishing they had the nerve to just ask; all gone."

A bot fly lazily buzzes by but Macky is thinking about Japan.

Puso un baile un junta, para una gran diversión.

"Cow, did you hear that? He said a rodent put on a dance for some great amusement.'"

Ba-badom ba-badom ba-badom ba-badom The four straight bass repeater kicks. Ba-badom, ba-badom, ba-badom, ba-badom. Ferrer and another vocalist start in, *Ay Candela, ay candela, candela me quemo ae.* Hear that cow? hear them say, 'Oh fire, fire, I'm burning.' Bovine, there is now actual space to do the Samba!

And again Bad Dandy is back with his left arm ready to take the oath•right touching the shoulder bade of Macky. Macky is back too, having smelled the rancid thoughts of Bad Dandy.

"Now cow, move and follow. One two three four. One two three four.

ba-badom ba-badom, ba-badom ba-badom."

Bad Dandy slides his left foot forward and does that ball exchange. He then slid his right to the back of his left, lifts up the transfers to the right then slides the left back two three.

De timbalero un ratón, que alegraba el campo un dia.

"Hear that one cow? 'He chose a mouse as his drummer, to play for the whole day.'" You take her hand and lead her to the dance floor. A step, and you two are in the jungle. *Un gato también venía, elegante y placentero, Buenas noches, compañero* a little more. The moon looms and shines on this couple. Each beat flashes Bad Dandy's grin deadlier.

"Keep up with the leader, idiot."

An elegant and amiable cat came along too, 'Good evening my friend' And the smell of the jungle comes into being. Lush tough bark trees grow. *Siempre dijo así el timbal* A bot fly is laying larvae on another puma. *He said to the drummer,* "Yes, true, can you hear? Are you focusing?" In several days time the larvae will eat the flesh of the puma away, killing it. *Para alguien aquí poder tocar, para descansar un poco. I can play too, and you can take a rest.*

And Macky thinks it could actually happen. They could be this close to Cuba.

"This can be yours, moo-moo." *Salió el ratón medio loco.* "Turns and turns and you two are naked and fucking on banana leaves, *The mouse left the room half-crazy,* thinking of doing unto others, *también voy a descansar.* as they have done onto you two, *now I'll have to go and rest!* the glory of this Elise, *Y el gato en su buen bailar, bailaba un danzón liviano.* The triumph. *And the cat played a lighthearted danzón in his delightful way.* Stop looking down, grass-grazer! The job, *El ratón se subió al guano, y dice* the home in the bush, *The mouse got up on the palm-tree roof and* lastly, her. *bien placentero:* It can all be yours, *announced politely:* cow, but first you must stomp. *¡Y ahora si quieren bailar, búsquense And now if you want to dance, find yourself another drummer!*

    "This is no imagination that I see here," and Band Dandy broke lose of Macky who thinks of being the leader. With her, cow. Not your imagination, *otro timbalero!* running away with you; stomp. *Ay candela, candela, candela me quemó aé.* Stomp damn you! *Oh fire, fire, fire, I'm burning!* Stomp, *Oye, Faustino Orama' y sus compañeros,* Elsie the cow, *Listen, Faustino Orama' and friends,* stomp, *necesito que me apaguen el fuego.* for the dance; *I need someone to put out the flames.* if you want her. *Margarita llama pronto a los bomberos para* And pick more fights, *Margarita call the fire-men quickly,* sometime. *que vengan a apagar el fuego.* If you want her as your bride." *to put out the flames.*

    Bad Dandy disappeared.

mama °Aaaay!   *Mama, ay!*

"I do, Bad Dandy."

Se le abre el entendimiento as Macky turned to walk home he realized that people, *She opens her mind,* had been staring at him since the restaurant fight, *La mujer cuando se agacha,* even following him into the alley. *When a woman bends over,* A woman is calling the cops. *Se le abre el entendimiento* He grabbed her phone. *she opens her mind. Y el hombre cuando la mira.* He didn't know she knew high karate. *When a woman bends over,* Bloody, *Se le para el pensamiento* limping away from the fight *His brain rises up,* Macky decides that in the future, *De tí me gusta una cosa,* if he is going to fight people, *I like one thing about you* it will be done from behind the, *Sin que me cueste trabajo,* steering wheel of a car, *It's not hard to see* like that guy Dandy told him about: Ronald, a man who could never really get it together.

Se quema, se quema, se quema, oye, mira   *He's burning, burning,*
burning, listen,

    me quemo, me quemo.   *look, I'm burning, I'm*
burning.

Mira que me quemo, oye, yo quiero

    seguir guarachando.

Oye se quema, se quema.

burning.

Look I'm burning

I can't stop myself.

Listen, he's burning, he's

4. NIGHT INTO DAY INTO NIGHT INTO DAY. BY ME: RONALD

Someone had broken into my car. Dang. Anyway, I got the car into one of the open bays or docks, whatever, at my studioliveworkwarehouse space. The night was dark and I was like, well Ronald, do ya wanna try to fix this up in the dark, in the parking lot, or do you want to have a go at it inside? Ronald, I said again, remember that that weirdo, O'Donell or something like that is still on the loose. Plus, he could have done this. Plus there might even be another weirdo group out here with dreams of becoming gods. Or just some serious freaks.

I decided to move the car into one of the open bays. That's what they call them out here but I think of it as an enclosed dock. I hate this place. The warehouse was a pillow factory back in the 20s, but had been renovated into almost kinda livable spaces. They do that a lot out here. Convert stuff. But they kept the docks intact so you could back a vehicle in. No privacy though. A few of my neighbors walked by. My neighbors are stupid. Most of them anyway. Because of them it took awhile to fit the plastic over the window.

Shattered plastic glass was on the seats, floorboard, everywhere and I had to scoop it out by hand. Harry walked by. I asked if he had seen anyone.

A lawbreaker, to be specific. That's why I just asked if he had seen or heard anything, saw anything, or if he had heard of someone else who had seen or heard anything. A dumb look stared back at me. I threw some glass on the floor and stepped on it. Next I opened the front passenger door and put my hand through where a window could perhaps be, ripping the plastic. Oops.

"OH. When did that happen, Ronny? Did someone break into your car there?"

"Yeah Harry, it happened maybe before I started fixing this here plastic to this here door."

" . . . did you see anything there, Ron?"

"Umm, no, if I had, I wouldn't have to ask you, right? And can you call me Ronald, my actual name?"

OH, papa, why do I put up with it?

"Well Ro, I haven't seen anything, ya know? But that happened to me too."

"Did you see them?"

"Huh?"

"Nothing."

"I gotta go. Bye R."

Another couple also asked if the car had been broken into.

"Why yes, Steve, it has. That's why I'm using plastic to cover up this here open space here and removing shattered glass from the front seats."

"Huh? Yeah, right Ron. Um, you know you can't use cardboard."

"I know. This is plastic. It's kinda opaque but it allows some light to pass."

"You see cardboard, you can't see out of it. I used cardboard."

I went back to clearing out my personal effects and Steve became a little more obnoxious by stepping down to continue. "As I was sayin, this is a great city. Well, we got the trash problem you know, litter. It's expensive. And we live in warehouses . . . wait, hybridity . . . where was I? Do I need to jack up the rent on my properties? Was that what I was talking about? Oh right, right. At least it ain't East Bay, ya know? Wait, oh right, I used this cardboard to fix a window on my truck once and didn't remember once and pulled out of a parking space and crunch! Right into another car. Wait, I hit him because I had backed up without looking. Use plastic."

I thanked him for the advice about the cardboard.

"Don't mention it. We gotta go do couple things now, Ro, but use plastic."

"Right. Say, have either of you seen anything suspicious lately? Like someone breaking into a car?"

"Huh?"

"Nothing."

The hooligans stole my notebooks, scarves, workshoes, berets, shoestrings, but they left my John Tesh *Winter Wonderland* CD, the radio and two cases of Diet Coke. Oh yeah, and they took my 40 ounces of coffee creamer. Bastards. I gulped one of the Cokes right then and there to show my defiance, but the dock gates were down so the effect was not very effective. I went to the restroom. When I got back there was a note left on the windshield:

Hey there, friend. I see you have had an
experience. We know, we all know. It's a shame. You
parked your car in a gravel lot but in a safe
neighborhood. But oh my, my boy the buts! Didn't
think of that when the music hit ya, did ya? Oh no,
slave to the rhythm and all that. Cheap well drinks
watered down with, water, expectations of doing the
electric waltz with a little tango were bumpin in
your head instead. Oh yes, your friends see pretty
good! Then you are coming back from shaking it,
listenin to DJ Ricky das Rickster! and something
feels amiss. More than it being dark out, more than

there being only a few stars out, garbage on the ground, a condom or two, no, something else. You went clubbin and you come back out and a window . . . is missing? Why do you suspect that? Paranoid? Perhaps you left it down? FAT CHANCE WITH GLASS RESTING ALONG THE FRONT PASSENGER SEAT! You are no longer a virgin, love. You are one of us now. If you want more, call this number: 1900-703-9543.

What a note! Who's DJ Ricky? Probably some murdering thug life type. Those people intimidate me. What's wrong with easy New Age music? Anyway, why were they using a 900 number! I hate those things. I'm kicking that habit. My fingers have already walked a long way with those numbers. Fornicated with them. But not any longer. I threw the note away, fixed my plastic and drove back to my matchbox apartment. Important people need at least two places to live. It was located in another county, all vanilla too, just like the brochure said. In the morning there was another note:

Hi. Don't be worried, friend. Call the number,

friend. We can help you get over this and regain
your selfworth, friend. It's a tragic, tragic thing,
losing a window. I know, we all know. Are you new
out here? You have an out of town license plate so,
so we know you don't have a very good support
system. Not out here anyway. It really, really,
behooves you, friend. Friend. Lastly, with a
superfund site so close to that space in the city,
don't you want a real side window?

I read this one with my mouth open just in case people were looking.
I don't like people but I need stimulation, which is why I use the numbers.
I'm a creature too! Ya know? I just don't like people! Is that so weird? So
much that I've had to move three times to keep the phone cops off my back?
With all that therapy I'm gonna take?

That happened awhile ago, when I was strong. Since then, once or
twice, I sighed over those white digits, even brushed against the 1 and 9 for no
good reason.

A week ago I went outside and there was another note. This one was in the outline of a phone pad. No it wasn't.


```
Do you have a job to go to? Do you have even
that much self-respect? Then why don't you stand for
something? They took from you and this is all you're
gonna do? What's it gonna take? Stand up for your
stupid rights! Call us, please. We can help you. We
are the right people and we even like you, maybe.
Call before we must leave messages on your answering
machine about this matter. Thank you. Friends.
```

It was still a 900 listing! I'm a machine! I'm not an animal! Wait, yeah I am. But what did they want from me? To stop my therapy? Yet they're right. What am I doing? Driving around with flapping rattling sheets on my hoop-ride, listening to the breeze glide through duct tape and dirty plastic. Plastic that expands and contracts depending on if you are opening or closing the door, it's way of saying, "here comes the cheap guy." And the therapy? Damming damnit to heaven, no therapy then! Is that the way then? Then fine, see if I care! But I was forced! Forced! The notes would go and on until I surrendered anyway, so I got in the right frame of mind. Yes, I listened to two then three busty hefty coeded women pour sticky stuff all over themselves. But I cringe at exploitation! (beep, beep beep beep) Uh, then, imagine that, I'm use to this number. No, they just all look and feel alike. (beep beep beep) They got sticky! Sticky? (beep beep beep beep) Holding one of their own down. Oh the inhumanity! Yes, yes touch the young one in the trio; touch her to, to, to clean her off! You other two heftiest girls spank me—I mean her, for being sooo sticky. "wap wap whap!" Yes, a little discipline is just the ticket to cure that girl—the line went silent.

"Hello horny toad, and welcome to the Naughty and the Corrected fantasy line. My name is Melanie and I see you have dialed my number. Do you have a personal I.D. code?"

"My palms are hairy and sweaty—"

"What? Wait, your number is coming up—"

"I mean no. I don't have an I. D. code."

"I see. Well, no problem, we can bill you by your phone number at three dollars a minute. If you do not want to go this route just say no in the next three seconds."

"I, um, am a recovering—"

The three seconds went by too soon. The clock began to tick away.

"Eww, and hi! What's your name? Mine is Melanie and I'm five-foot five, red-brunette and like aerobics. I wear thong backs at home and have a pair with me. Should I put them on?"

"Hehe, I'm really the sweaty horny Rony back from—"

"Horny Rony! I knew it! Wierdo."

"No Melanie, this is official business! Let me explain."

"Explain my ass! Just listen to the recording."

If you want to hear more about three girls, a paddle, and a gallon of sticky goo, press two. If you want to talk to someone about the note, press three and give the password, which is: clip'em. If you want to hear about three precocious nectars being ice-creamed and cherried, press . . . .

I pressed the um, wrong button. All of the wrong buttons. Lastly, I figured out the right one after, um, listening to the nectars being cheeried. Again. Oh mother do I need discipline for my transgressions. Badly. I need to press two again, but only because of my naughtiness.

*   *   *

I'm a member now, though a neophyte with a sore bottom. To get a nickname and really be in the loop you have to prove your worth four times. Me, I showed them my long distance bill and they said, "Wow. Okay, Brother Ronald, just do one big thing." I had been told most members go this route.

Would my big thing be violent? You bet,but I didn't want to get caught. The law out here says it's no big deal that thieves break into your car, but running them over is a homicide if you do it right. If not, it's just vehicular manslaughter. Whatever. But here we are in a parking lot and on a mission.

Me and Carrot Top are here in a Ford Festiva—close to a cardboard cutout of an '87 El Camino, a sturdy vehicle if ever there were one. We parked three car lengths away. I'm scrunched down in the driver's seat using a penlight to write with. It's nighttime. Carrot Top is cheering me on. I'm the hero, ya know? This isn't our first time trying to do a big thing. Before this plan we tried to run them down before they got on a commuter train. Well, they got on the train anyway.

We were slumped down in an unmarked car late one night. It was dark then too. The hooligans were thinking of vandalizing the cut out Hyundai Sonata we had planted. They decided not to. These people have no class or taste. But we had a mission! That's what Carrot Top said too. So I hopped up, started the Yugo and gunned it right at them! It stalled out. But! It started again, wheezing with thick blue white smoke farting out from under the hood and tailpipe. It lurched and bucked lurched and whined and kicked up to a decent 5/8 miles per hour and!

Stalled.

Out.

We fled the scene; justice denied.

Even worse was the order to appear in front of the disciplinary committee. We met in the studioliveworkwarehouse basement.

"Brother Ronald, you have failed at your latest attempt."

"Yes, but, bu the vehicle we had—"

"I don't see how blaming such a weapon of mass destruction is going to save you, Brother Ronald."

"But Madam Chairwoman, it, it was a Yugo! It didn't even have a speaker in the dash! You all couldn't get me a Ford Festiva? How is it—" Hiss hiss hisssess!

Hisses and car fresheners were thrown at me. I had stirred the group indeed! What to do? I looked at them, crestfallen, "I accept full blame." They quieted down. I could feel Carrot Top cheering me on. "In my exuberance to clip the hooligans I opened her up too soon. We were both too excited, we were both too premature in our actions. I beg everyone's understanding for the enemy was right there! I am a man and I got needs!

"It all started with the Sears and Roebuck catalogs. The Christmas issue. Next I moved on to JC Penny's, but used Montgomery Wards when I felt like slumming, yeah. The ink would come off on my fingers and smear the pages so I would throw some talc on my fingertips and tickle my jungle serpent! The bliss of it all! But pages don't have voices to interact with so I bought this doll that—" Carrot Top coughed and seemed to not be watching, not cheering me on anymore. They were all staring at me, touching themselves. Madam Chairwoman wiped her brow before speaking.

"We will give you one more chance. If you fail this time though, you will have to begin all over."

"You mean with calling 900 numbers?"

"Yes Brother Ronald, plus you'll have to download the wet naughty from the Miss Jackson file."

"We will be successful this time Madam Chair. Why? I have a dream."

"But if not it's back to the phones for you, Ronald!"

"Is that a guarantee, Madam Chairwoman?"

"Yes, it is. Now assume the position."

"Yes, Madam Chair."

From the crowd, "Spank him good!"

Then the spanking began. Whaps whaps on the bottom, oh it was delicious, I have to say. Then, oh yes I got a chance to use a lifeline and tag Beatrice in; she's the one who had said to spank me good. And it was her turn, here, in the bowels of the warehouse where the dust settled years ago, and the oil and grit had sealed up all the cracks. Underground with all the accountants and lawyers and other people who needed to wear cloaks for those activities would get them fired from their day jobs. This was worth it? But I am in a gang now, plus I have some free phone minutes.

That was how we got here, on this creep, waiting for the El Camino to be vandalized. Just the two of us. Tensed.

The street crickets are holding their breath in anticipation. Crouched, no one can see me. There is nothing out here, nothing but warehouses on both sides on the street. And litter. The no parking signs are tagged with gang signs. Drunks stumble past me, talking to their imaginary friends.

The wind blows chickie bird smells from the local chicken shack. It creeps in, mostly from the rusted out floorboard, up my nose, then down to my stomach, which grumbles. I can even see the grease from the shack leaking into sewer drains, taking all the spilt liqueur and wrong lottery tickets with it. In the distance you can see large luxurious mucky muck condominiums but this is a desolate place. Why do I have to be here? Am I ever going to do more than this?

The sound of the pen is very loud. Carrot Top is sitting on the dash, all still, almost a doll and not a little friend. We have to be good tonight to get what we have come for done. If not it's back to endure the naughty Miss Jackson file and then maybe Flabio and the adventures of Dorothy as she gets it from behind. Limousine liberal style. Smut rules.

*   *   *

The sun will be up soon. Damn if the hooligans have not shown up. But they will, they will. Until then, until I become a full member the plastic must stay up. I can't get the window replaced with the special "can't touch this" formula until I have proven myself. I'm no longer a virgin, neither is the car, but to become a full member one must complete the journey and clip clip clip'em!

It's almost 10:30 in the AM and the idea of chronicling my night saga at night is real problematic in the daytime. Hot. The sun is bearing down and the birds have gone on the cut out. I don't know, I don't know. Carrot Top is no longer sitting up but lying down. I could lay her on the backseat and do speed dial. Then what? I know, and that's why my bags are packed and any busy street of pedestrians will do. And hey, wasn't that why I'm not using my car?

CHAPTER FIVE

Twist and shout

Chubby Checker

1. BATTLE CRY

Fuck the dentist, bailin straight from a root canal! A young tooth got it bad cause he's brown, Yeeaaaaahh!

Diary entry

Dear Diary, my jaw was still sore but we went to the airport today to watch watch watch—anyway. The people. They did not see me. They saw Bad Dandy in my arms. He wore a furry animal costume and I looked like a nice tyke waiting for his little food gobbler buddy to come back home. But no child should have to come to my place. It's not too small but there is a lot of food NOT TO BE TOUCHED! HA! Liar! I threw it all away diary, you know that.

It was a nice airport. Lots of interracial walking around: Asian security guards and young white women stewardesses. White manboy pilots who haven't seen any real work, of course. Guess what else Dandy told me? The colored fly Trans Chitlins America, a subsidiary of the New Pan Africa Corporation. The browns fly Latino airlines. Dandy said I could Get the latest news about the Coca-Cola el presidente whilst listening to hot debates over Ricky Martin's Chicanoness.

Bad Dandy also said the Protestant white folks from yesteryear won and all the folks of color with character got shot and this is why we are where we are. Bad Dandy has taught me a lot of things I

didn't know about the Protestants though I worked
for them.

We left when Bad Dandy wanted to go.
Good thing because I kept hearing munching.
That sound again.

The good Sam and Macky have had a falling out.

2. MACKY WRITES WHY HE MUST CONTINUE ON:

Mylifeisshit.Mylifeisshit.My life is shit.My life is shit.My life is shit.My life is shit. Mylifeisshit.Mylifeisshit.My life is shit.My life is shit.My life is shit.My life is shit

Mylifeisshit.Mylifeisshit.My life is shit.My life is shit.My life is shit.My life is shit. Mylifeisshit.Mylifeisshit.My life is shit.My life is shit.My life is shit.My life is shit

Mylifeisshit.Mylifeisshit.My life is shit.My life is shit.My life is shit.My life is shit. Mylifeisshit.Mylifeisshit.My life is shit.My life is shit.My life is shit.My life is shit

Mylifeisshit.Mylifeisshit.My life is shit.My life is shit.My life is shit.My life is shit. Mylifeisshit.Mylifeisshit.My life is shit.My life is shit.My life is shit.My life is shit

Mylifeisshit.Mylifeisshit.My life is shit.My life is shit.My life is shit.My life is shit. Mylifeisshit.Mylifeisshit.My life is shit.My life is shit.My life is shit.My life is shit

Mylifeisshit.Mylifeisshit.My life is shit.My life is shit.My life is shit.My life is shit. Mylifeisshit.Mylifeisshit.My life is shit.My life is shit.My life is shit.My life is shit

Mylifeisshit.Mylifeisshit.My life is shit.My life is shit.My life is shit.My life is shit. Mylifeisshit.Mylifeisshit.My life is shit.My life is shit.My life is shit.My life is shit

Mylifeisshit.Mylifeisshit.My life is shit.My life is shit.My life is shit.My life is shit. Mylifeisshit.Mylifeisshit.My life is shit.My life is shit.My life is shit.My life is shit

Mylifeisshit.Mylifeisshit.My life is shit.My life is shit.My life is shit.My life is shit. Mylifeisshit.Mylifeisshit.My life is shit.My life is shit.My life is shit.My life is shit

Mylifeisshit.Mylifeisshit.My life is shit.My life is shit.My life is shit.My life is shit. Mylifeisshit.Mylifeisshit.My life is shit.My life is shit.My life is shit.My life is shit

Mylifeisshit.Mylifeisshit.My life is shit.My life is shit.My life is shit.My life is shit. Mylifeisshit.Mylifeisshit.My life is shit.My life is shit.My life is shit.My life is shit

Mylifeisshit.Mylifeisshit.My life is shit.My life is shit.My life is shit.My life is shit. Mylifeisshit.Mylifeisshit.My life is shit.My life is shit.My life is shit.My life is shit

Mylifeisshit.Mylifeisshit.My life is shit.My life is shit.My life is shit.My life is shit. Mylifeisshit.Mylifeisshit.My life is shit.My life is shit.My life is shit.My life is shit

Mylifeisshit.Mylifeisshit.My life is shit.My life is shit.My life is shit.My life is shit. Mylifeisshit.Mylifeisshit.My life is shit.My life is shit.My life is shit.My life is shit

Mylifeisshit.Mylifeisshit.My life is shit.My life is shit.My life is shit.My life is shit. Mylifeisshit.Mylifeisshit.My life is shit.My life is shit.My life is shit.My life is shit

Mylifeisshit.Mylifeisshit.My life is shit.My life is shit.My life is shit.My life is shit. Mylifeisshit.Mylifeisshit.My life is shit.My life is shit.My life is shit.My life is shit

Mylifeisshit.Mylifeisshit.My life is shit.My life is shit.My life is shit.My life is shit. Mylifeisshit.Mylifeisshit.My life is shit.My life is shit.My life is shit.My life is shit

Mylifeisshit.Mylifeisshit.My life is shit.My life is shit.My life is shit.My life is shit. Mylifeisshit.Mylifeisshit.My life is shit.My life is shit.My life is shit.My life is shit

Mylifeisshit.Mylifeisshit.My life is shit.My life is shit.My life is shit.My life is shit. Mylifeisshit.Mylifeisshit.My life is shit.My life is shit.My life is shit.My life is shit

Mylifeisshit.Mylifeisshit.My life is shit.My life is shit.My life is shit.My life is shit. Mylifeisshit.Mylifeisshit.My life is shit.My life is shit.My life is shit.My life is shit

Mylifeisshit.Mylifeisshit.My life is shit.My life is shit.My life is shit.My life is shit. Mylifeisshit.Mylifeisshit.My life is shit.My life is shit.My life is shit.My life is shit

Mylifeisshit.Mylifeisshit.My life is shit.My life is shit.My life is shit.My life is shit. Mylifeisshit.Mylifeisshit.My life is shit.My life is shit.My life is shit.My life is shit

Mylifeisshit.Mylifeisshit.My life is shit.My life is shit.My life is shit.My life is shit. Mylifeisshit.Mylifeisshit.My life is shit.My life is shit.My life is shit.My life is shit

Mylifeisshit.Mylifeisshit.My life is shit.My life is shit.My life is shit.My life is shit. Mylifeisshit.Mylifeisshit.My life is shit.My life is shit.My life is shit.My life is shit

Mylifeisshit.Mylifeisshit.My life is shit.My life is shit.My life is shit.My life is shit. Mylifeisshit.Mylifeisshit.My life is shit.My life is shit.My life is shit.My life is shit

Mylifeisshit.Mylifeisshit.My life is shit.My life is shit.My life is shit.My life is shit. Mylifeisshit.Mylifeisshit.My life is shit.My life is shit.My life is shit.My life is shit

Mylifeisshit.Mylifeisshit.My life is shit.My life is shit.My life is shit.My life is shit. Mylifeisshit.Mylifeisshit.My life is shit.My life is shit.My life is shit.My life is shit

Mylifeisshit.Mylifeisshit.My life is shit.My life is shit.My life is shit.My life is shit. Mylifeisshit.Mylifeisshit.My life is shit.My life is shit.My life is shit.My life is shit

Mylifeisshit.Mylifeisshit.My life is shit.My life is shit.My life is shit.My life is shit. Mylifeisshit.Mylifeisshit.My life is shit.My life is shit.My life is shit.My life is shit

Mylifeisshit.Mylifeisshit.My life is shit.My life is shit.My life is shit.My life is shit. Mylifeisshit.Mylifeisshit.My life is shit.My life is shit.My life is shit.My life is shit.My life is shit.My life is Mylifeisshit.Mylifeisshit.My life is shit.My life is shit.My life is shit.My life is shit. Mylifeisshit.Mylifeisshit.My life is shit.My life is shit.My life is shit.My life is

shit   shit   shit   shit   shit   shit

3. TO BEAT THE MAN OR TO BE THE MAN

Drums

Percussion

Done Prettily

To Chaos

Black then white are all I see, in my infancy.

The falling out happened on a clear day when you could see forever.

Red and yellow then came to be, reaching out to me.

Macky had put that "Lateralis" song on again. He turned it up. The Good Sam only listens to string recordings you know.

Macky knows that Sam does not like groups like *Tool. Lets me see.*

Macky was in the kitchen clutching the sink. Standing, leaning back, his mouth wide open, hoping, praying this would ease the pain. He uses the remote to turn the volume up again. A few minutes later a Miss Sarah Gilmore bangs on the door. Macky stumbled to the left and opened it.

As below, so above and beyond, I imagine.

"Oh my," and he pulled her in. Sam was standing now in the living room partly hidden by the wall, watching.

Miss Gilmore, "Macky, I think you should let me go. If you do I'll get you something for the pain."

Dandy was looking at all this from the outside. His boy was finally showing some promise! *Drawn beyond the lines of reason.*

Push the envelope. Watch it bend.

"Somethin for the pain? Cause I'm in pain? That's why I behave this way? Please promise."

Dandy fell out the tree and rested on the grass wondering why must it be so hard.

"Yes Macky yes, I can get you pain relievers, if that's why you're grimacing."

"Pamprin, Miss Gilmore?"

"Call me Sarah, please, and yes, Pamprin. It helped before, right?"

"Okay. Go get, please." He released her.

> *Over thinking, over analyzing separates the body*
> *from the mind.*

> *Withering my intuition, missing opportunities and I must*

> *Feed my will to feel my moment . . . .*

She ran upstairs thinking of how Sam said he could handle him. Now the little maniac had taken over Sam's place and was depleting her medicine cabinet. She was taking all that into account when she opened her front door and saw her dream man, but he was not soothing, this time.

"Good evening, my good lady. My name is not important but I assure you as I could pluck your eyes out and step on them, if you do not leave this place this instant without stopping to help my cow, you will feel and feel things your mother could have never prepared you for."

Black then white are all I see, in my infancy.

Red and yellow then came to be, reaching out to me.

Lets me see there is so much more

and beckons me to look through to these infinite possibilities..

Sarah backed out into the hallway. Bad Dandy handed over her purse.

"I put a few extra bills in there just in case you wanted to go see a show. I think there's a gruff sounding fellow singing at the 'Lounge of Last Resorts.' I put the address in your little appointment book."

"You, you're real. But you do not come into my dreams anymore," she says.

"I will, after you have been swallowed. Three weeks or something like that, yes?"

"Three and a half, sir. And what is your name, pray tell."

Over thinking, over analyzing separates the body from the mind.

Withering my intuition leaving all these opportunities

behind.

And they said it together. "Bad Dandy."

4. BACK AT SAM'S PLACE

"Macky," Sam groaned. A rolled up section of Metro in his hands. In the middle of the roll-up are sharp pieces of pottery. Actually they a sticking out of the paper.

"Macky, you ought not have scared Sarah like that. You should have learned to mind me in my house, Macky."

Macky didn't care much, or at least not now. He was in a little pain. But he did notice that Sarah and this Good Sam never went out, or ate intimate dinners in Good Sam's place. Or that would have went through his mind, he would have taken that into account if the pain wasn't pressing him. It was so he moved to his right, back into the kitchen, hands on the sink, making sounds to gods, "Please stop the pain," whispering as mucus ran down his throat. Macky was doing mouthing stretches, trying to ease the stress, even.

His body was breaking down from the trauma of not eating. He was shrinking and his mouth wanted to oblige but the nerves cried out that his mouth could not shrink anymore without food. Paradox. But there were no other ways to transcend, were there?

"Macky," as Sam walked clockwise from his hiding area in the shadow of the living room to the middle then left of the living room, thinking Sarah would be back soon. He spied Macky pleading but Sarah, she must be protected from this strange man. But he looked so defensless.

"Why must I suffer, Sam? How much suffering? I ache with this. It has a hold on me. I cannot take anymore, I can't." His voice pitched up and down on the vowels, i, e, o, and a and u. "I want to be good, transcend, but this was taking too much from me. Always too much."

"Macky! Look at me, dear boy. I feel your pain might be—"

"Shut up! I can't hear the words if you're gonna blather now can I?"

Sam looked at Macky who continued turning his head back and forth, looking for the right spot. His eyes were red and his skin clammy. His hands were wet from crying into them. He trembled and a voice came through.

Macky turned to see Sam now easing closer to him.

I embrace my desire.

Sam brought the newspaper down on Macky's forehead.

> *To feel inspired, to fathom the power,*
>
> *to witness the beauty, to bathe in the fountain,*
>
> *to swing on the spiral*
>
> *of our divinity and still be a human.*

"Boy, I have had what I believe is enough. I take you in and you throw away my food and scare my woman." Sam brought the paper up backhand style this time; the pottery now in smaller shards. The lick hit right at the root of the pains.

Macky, for a few moments only heard the guitars and quick drums moving together. Then that about desire and Macky heard the quieting of the music. The lead singer whispered lines of desire. Sam continued to strike Macky, now with his fists. The floor was yellow linoleum and the pottery pieces looked nice there. More pulsating rifting guitars and Macky grabbed a piece of concrete he had placed atop the refrigerator. Macky sang along.

With my feet upon the ground.

I move myself between the sounds,

and open wide to suck it in,

As he bashed Sam over and over until Sam fell to the floor.

I feel it move across my skin.

Sam crawled into the bedroom then bathroom with Macky still signing along in the kitchen.

I'm reaching for the random or what ever will

bewilder me.

And following our will and wind

we may just go where no one's been.

We'll ride the spiral to the end

and may just go where no one's been.

Spiral out. Keep going, going.

Spiral out. Keep going, going . . .

And when the song stopped Macky went into the bathroom and killed Sam.

5. ENTRIES AND ACCEPTANCE

I can decorate Like Bad Dandy

Dear Diary, I made a poem:
This Good Sam painted the walls black and had red
Marble furniture. The rug now has shards in it from
the furniture. Lime-green cardboard Arizona tea
boxes now litter the kitchen floor. In the bathroom
the mirror, the nightstand, vase and the other
bedroom crap is now broken. A draft tickles the
sheer curtain and behind is a broken man.

Diary entry

Dear diary, I smell. Plus no Pamprin. I have
not taken a bath since I freed myself. Wrestled my
freedom back! It's wonderful but I just don't know.
I have some words but words are failing me . . .
no matter. I am going to change change change. Bad
Dandy told me my way was without bathing. I like Bad

Dandy except he does get me beat up sometimes but I trust him for he promised me he'd help me meet her. The thought of her. The idea of her makes me viral, oh, she's precious! And luscious and small. I wonder what she smells like? I wonder if she will want to die together. Maybe. It's about time I beat off. Me and My Bad Tooth are patching up some things. I want to leave, run, but what if the mouths find and eat me? Wait, I'm ruining my mood for whackin. Here I go! I gotta ask what was Bleeding Kansas about.

Diary entry

Dear diary, I watched Bad Dandy lift a car onto the flat bed. It wasn't mine but this late Good Sam wasn't gonna be usin it either so I got attached to it. Bad Dandy was so displeased with that he spat at me. But why didn't he see the likeness? The car was like me, you know? "This will teach you a lesson," he said. "This will toughen you up," he said. "Remember Bleeding Kansas," he said.

But I went soft inside. Bad Dandy was my friend. The only one in the whole world I could count on for truth and wisdom and here he was towing my wheels away.

I watched the apartment gate open. Dandy, with his tow-cap on, hauled it upon the bed, goosed the engine a couple of times then drove away. I went back in and reclined on the owner's body. It's okay because I've wrapped it up so the smell wouldn't attract flies. If I wanted the car back, I was really gonna have to totally listen to him now. I also told Bad Tooth we couldn't be as close as I thought we were going to be. It doesn't really matter. Not anymore. I have crossed even further

diary, not that I want to, but what if I thought about going back to the lab?

Diary entry

Dear diary, today during my morning run Bad Dandy drove past me in that tow-truck! He wasn't towing anything this time but he did throw a couple of beer cans at me. He's training me I guess. I'm a true pedestrian now. Until I do right by him. Or go back to the lab. Can I do that? Or would I like being eaten? I want Bad I I want Bad Dandy to be eaten. I don't want to be eaten. I just might quit this. I need a sign.

Diary entry

Dear diary, I'm so happy! This afternoon I woke to a letter that said I was lean enough! Plus tickets for the train so it's off I go! It read:

Elsie, Cow, lean and stupid but would forage

Pick up your udders and your tiny little courage.

Run to the station with fury

and flea,

        there is another place where

you need to be.

        It's dirty, bloody, this land

of bills,

        if you think of pleasure, none

here, but liqueur spills.

        So steel your courage Elsie

        and please come and see me.

        Before I fucking kill you.

II

Middle Passage

CHAPTER SIX

People are strange, when you're a stranger

The Doors

1. ALL ABOARD

The train station was two miles from where Macky was laid up at. Five minutes into walking he wished for a ride and showed some thumb. Then calf. Both. Shin. Both lower legs plus feet in socks. Then no socks. No luck. Finally the station was in sight.

Macky was so happy he failed to notice the thing in the ticket both. He was eight feet tall, had the head of a pufferfish and the body of a lanky guy. Instead of toes he had hooves. The thing had yelled out not to touch the leopard as he checked Mackey's ticket and Mackey opened his diary.

Diary entry

Dear diary, as I walked into the station I thought about this place having such an old terminal. I think Bad Tooth is just along for the ride now. We aren't even business partners anymore. But the throb! Sometimes my nose burns, the inside, the gooey part of the nostrils because of the pain. And now I wait for the train to come into the station for my special trip.

It's just that recently I wondered back to the labcoaters. Who doesn't want to be all they can? Be a team of one? The possibilities of one. Am I looking for an out? Can I get back to my home? I think I heard something munching on a girl.

This place needs to be remodeled, diary. Flaking brown cracked walls that match brown concrete floors do not move me. Nor do these attached gold and red chairs. I am not the only one here, either. People are sitting all around me. Two

German women are talking about why one should not pet any anything from the cat family. To each his own, I say. Oh oh, the one I think works in a barbershop, her tag says so, anyway, is looking at me. On the next line it says her name is Glende. I pretend not to notice. She walks by my chair, tisking me. How rude.

Oh man, this newly married romantic couple to my right is singing and kissing and singing, "I couldn't be ten days older ~ and still belong. I walk down the road with my eyes closed and I still expect to be able to see. I walk down the road with my eyes closed and know that he will walk with me, me." Onward Christian Soldiers? Don't I deserve better? Oh, what's that I hear from this older couple?

"We did it John, we finally ditched the kids."

"Yes goodness Emily, we did it! Now all we gotta do is get on the next train out of here and start living proper. Freedom is so close that I think I love you."

"Oh John, ditto."

2. LOOKY LOOKY

The train pulled up. Macky had to porter his bag. He got on. Aboard he heard new languages. He sat behind two white cowboys next to two Korean girls who kept screeching and sighing in his direction. Everyone was in jeans and white tee's but no Disney logos. The Korean girls stopped looking at him and started playing with their phone.

Macky would really love to have hot Bostonian sex with them, he wrote as much in his diary. He panted and wrote. He sipped on his Schlitz and Diet Pepsi for perspective and nutrition. He wandered if Bad Dandy would approve. He chirped and wanted them but the Mennonite girl looked pretty good too but what do they know about the ways of love? The Korean girls looked at his pants queer like. Oh, their loudass voices were making him sick though! But Frenchie? She's his true love! Burp, and he passed out.

"Get up, ugly, the next one is on track 6."

Macky thanked the conductor, got off, sneezed, and when he looked up noticed another train on a platform above. A pig standing on her hinds in a blanket wearing a beret waved at him to her podium and said, "If you are willing and bold, sprat, crawl under my podium and up the stairs behind me."

He looked behind her. The steps looked liquidy. Something flowed down them. Then Tooth throbbed telling him to hurry or someone else would notice how bad the pain was.

"Madam pig, I accept that path . . . is there anything else I should know?"

"Yes, sprat. When you get to the top of the platform, you will have five more chances to turn back. All you have to do is not pet the leopard, for example. But if you pet the leopard, even once, you ugly bug, you are then, then, on the fast track you have been seeking. You ugly bug. Unless you listen wrongly."

He thanked her and crawled under her podium. It had that wet beer wheat roll on a warm day smell.

CHAPTER SEVEN

I'm so in love with you

Al Green

1. A MEDITATIVE SOUL

Too hard my heart

I'll cut off my tongue

The things I've said

The things I've done

Blind Willie Johnson

Bad Dandy with orange gums has always had trouble finding gainful office employment. He stole the right resumes, snatched the right suits and other business trinkets, but just did not fit in. He even went so far as killing parts of the interviewers' family and holding the rest captive as bargaining chips.

He never actually held anyone, actually. He never wanted to buy them food or give them water so he always hacked them up and left them in landfills.

At interviews he would get bored and go to sleep. Once he forgot that he filled his briefcase with knives and when his interviewer started talking about himself as the company, Bad Dandy decided to slash his aureoles off. He did too, leaping on top of the fellow, knocking him out his chair and straddling him. Bad Dandy then got nostalgic.

"I used to creep into tenements. In those days I only had a monogrammed handkerchief and a hammer. Not true, really, for I had a boot-knife but I simply refuse to tell you all my secrets—stop struggling during the narrative."

Bad Dandy looked up and out the windows. It was a clear, warm, lively, blue day. He even wondered about all this duty and promotion stuff. But only for a few seconds. Then back to the office being beige. The walls, ceiling, even the carpet. A little red would do fine as it slowly ran from Mr. Stanislowski, known as Stan the man. Stan would be a decent bleeder, Dandy thought. He was right.

"Anyway, Stan, I had a hanky and a hammer. The hanky in your mouth now is the very one. Well, to make a long story shorter, I'm gonna leave now. I'm taking the hanky, my knives and a hammer you have not seen yet. If the police start looking for me because of this, your family will see my hammer. Okay? Okay."

Stan seemed to have passed out. Dandy looked around Stan's desk, no pictures of wife and kiddies. No leverage. "Well now, I guess it's plan 'B' for me and Stanley." Dandy threw himself and Stan out the window. The difference was that Stanley's body fell five floors onto a bus. Bad Dandy, ever the crawler, had grabbed the ledge above, briefcase between his legs, and pulled himself up. Sitting he then took the straps out of the case, fastened, cinched them to his back and scampered up to the roof. Gone. My goodness, when would his protégé get up to speed?

2. AL GREEN PLAYED ON

He did not have stabbing in mind at all when he went to the theater interview; he went with pink gums, colored contact lenses, and clunky shoes, manicured nails and took the food from his teeth. Undyed hair, too.

He did all this because there was someone he had fallen in love with. She was the same height as he with a long face and pointy chin. Long, shiny, strong, black hair that made little sounds when she ran her hands through it. Her teeth were straight and white and she did not have any meat in them. She laughed at his jokes. She wore clunky shoes. That's why he did this one. Besides wanting to think about something else besides the fact that Macky seemed prone to concrete, not the best weapon of choice for a killer.

I, I'm so in love with you.

Whatever you want to do is all right with me.

One night, at the theater job, something happened that made Bad Dandy decide to just hang out in his refrigerator until Macky came over.

It was around midnight and he as the projectionist was escorting the cashier upstairs. Nice girl with that mini and black stockings on but still nothing like the Elvira who had hired him. They were going up the back way,

Rebecca demanded, when there was a knock. There was a door at the bottom of the stairs, but an emergency door.

"Don't open it, Rebecca," from Dandy, hands full of cashier boxes.

She looked at him but jumped when the knocks became louder.

"Don't open it, Rebecca! Upstairs is where we should be. This is a job for the proper authorities."

"Yeah, O'Donnell, right."

She opened the door.

A kid peeked his head through.

"Get back Rebecca, back!" Bad Dandy sprinted to the door, trying to shove it closed but the boy sprayed him with ammonia. Bad Dandy fell back.

"Becky," from the boy, "who's this mule?"

"He's the projectionist, Josh. What are we gonna do? Can't have any witnesses."

Joshua flipped a blade out. "Sorry man, but that'd be life."

Bad Dandy, in his head, said this never happened. He was really in his fridge.

Joshua came at him, knife out. Bad Dandy blocked the upward swing, twisted his wrist to get the knife and threw him down, Bad Dandy on top, cutting at the boy's abdomen.

Loving you forever is what I need.

Let me be the one you come running to.

"Listen to me idiot," Bad Dandy whispered and in the background he heard something, hopefully sirens, maybe an ambulance. And if nothing else she should be horse whipped, he thought. "Don't struggle and—" Rebecca heard another knock. She went to the door. Joshua's buddy strode in. "Tell your boy to not take another step or a slash on the right of your neck is next, Joshua."

"Agaaeeale foo uu or," came out of the boy's mouth.

Bad Dandy did it as the other boy came at him. Bad Dandy swirled, knelt next to Joshua to punch the boy with "Mordecai" on his sweatshirt in the scrotum. Bad Dandy stood then kicked him making him fall backward. Bad Dandy walked over and broke his right arm. Rebecca kept screaming. Bad Dandy then dragged Mordecai over to Joshua. Bad Dandy thought for sure that sound was something in the distance and was fading. "No," as it came back into focus. Plus his refrigerator.

He loomed over Mordecai grinning, "Mordecai, you stop your moaning before I donkey sex you." The moans stopped.

Standing over Joshua, "You called me a mule and I am not. My parents were from the land of bogs and mists, idiot boy, the both of you! Why have you made me do this to you? . . . I will forgive you though, if you will just continue to live."

He knelt over Joshua to feel his pulse, putting his hand under him and noticing the blood drowning the red carpet.

"Please, you fool, please live. Oh! You are so young; fight death and live. For just one more day. I know of an organization that would welcome you." The sounds come closer, again making the refrigerator fade out of view. The sound was not an ambulance. Words were being sung on an eight-track.

Let's, let's stay together. Lovin' you whether,

whether times are good or bad, happy or sad.

"Live live live village idiot!"

But the boy refused. Bad Dandy walked out the emergency door. Rebecca continued to scream. When is Macky going to get out here?

CHAPTER EIGHT

But I'm on the outside

Staind

1. SNOW LEOPARDS AND TIME

At the top of the platform Macky heard a muffled train from the east coming down the rail. Muffled thump thumps, thump thumps. He shivered for the temperature had fallen. He was also too busy thinking to wonder about the soft footsteps that turned to the pURRing sound behind him and the snow leopard that smiled up at him. He stuck out his right hand. The leopard took a few steps back. He took two more steps toward her. The leopard trotted down the platform. He ran after. The beast ran a little faster and so did he. Chase the cat!

"Come back," as Macky threw his head back and hands forward to run faster down the platform, chasing the cat.

*   *   *

Then it happened.

*   *   *

The night turned warm again. Cicadas creaked or tweaked with the crickets doing the same thing. The moon smiled redly. Macky took his jacket off, drapping it onto the floor which was no longer concrete. Gravel, instead. Crickets and insects made new sounds. New sounds. He smelled as his cologne and deodorant ran down his sides, back, and thighs. He took his shirt off. Modernity was again, just a theory.

Birds, swamp birds flapped overhead, eating away this civilization; they were the langoliers for this place.

A hanging tree full of potential defilers of wholesome women stared at him.

The leopard ran fast enough to be two feet away from being petted. The trees had gotten taller taller thicker dense grass, real grass from Georgia,

Kentucky; the South was now underfoot. Big forest bugs bit him in the face but there was no stopping now. Hairy chested he yanked his belt off and threw it at the leopard. Missed and he fought the need to slow down to a jog. The snow leopard realized it and the distance stayed the same.

An alligator murmured as rain filled a waddy. Somewhere. Florida? Macky kicked off both shoes yanked off sock and pant. The leopard slowed. Then underwear. The cat stopped and Macky stumbled down next to her. His sweat pooled, drenching the little rocks under him. He looked up and didn't see any stars. The moon was full, shining. Loud bugs humped and chirped.

The cat purred and rubbed against him. No concrete. No pocket. He touched poof! gray smoke. When Macky cleared the smoke a train came to a stop before him. The doors opened. A new set of clothes hung from a rusty hanger just inside the car. The dark clothes, sniff, pe-u, needed to be washed then burned. At one time these were fresh red pants, new Vans, and an "I left My Wallet in San Francisco" sweatshirt.

* * *

The front of the train, the engine car, looked bigger than the rest, bulbous even. A tree stump turned into steps so he could board. He boarded.

He put the clothes on. He did not think about the line on the post-it on the sweatshirt: All hope abandon, ye who enter here!

2. CRAZY CABOOSES

The Quitter

Macky finished dressing and looked up and down the car and saw no one. Just smells smells smells. Plus an old bald trembling man. The train moved west. Macky sat across from the old man. As he did the old man grinned at him. The old bald man looked up, smiled, "Come sit next to me, sonny boy. I'm supposed to show you somethin."

Macky raised an eyebrow to the old man patting the bench with his right hand and decided to see if anyone else were looking at them. No, so he got up and sat next to the old bald man in the pith helmet, long sleeve white cotton shirt, khakis shorts, and boots. Macky took him to be some big game hunter in love with the Hemingway way of having the natives take you into the bush, carry your guns, water, food, carry you, tell you where the prey was and watch you hunt it down. Elephant, rhino, tiger tiger, burning bright.

"Eh old man, what's up?"

The old man flashed his pointy teeth, his tongue danced on the tips of those good needles.

"Quittin boy, quittin. That's what's up."

"I'm going—"

The old man grabbed Macky's right hand, pinning it to the seat, all the time looking forward.

"But quittin's not a bad thing. Do you understand me? It's worse."

"What?"

With the old man's right hand the old, bald man leaned over to grabbed a book from his satchel. A hardback with a hard green scaly leather cover and backing. The pages blared white. The train shimmied and the wind whispered showtime.

The train rocked back and forth. The lights blinked with the whispering of showtime.

*   *   *

The veins on the old man's head stretched his face turning the thin areas around his cheeks, chin, and temples red. White teeth and black tongue. Black gums. All this did not matter because when the man opened his book to page one light shown as the lights in the car went out.

*   *   *

In the dark Macky tried to get up three times. On the third try the old man's left hand over Macky's right became a glove a size too small then dripped through the seat anchoring itself to the floor. The bald man then detached it at his wrist and blew on it. Macky wanted to groan. Macky wanted to leave. What do you do when a hand keeps you down? Smile. There you have it: Smile. Macky did, waiting for the bald man's story to take the hurt from his hand.

The train raised up a few feet then dipped down downs and down.

The bald man looked straight ahead. So did Macky.

"I taught huntin for somethin, son. Preached it. They looked up to me because of that, most did, I suppose. I still do not know which ones in particular mind you, for I did not know myself then, or maybe I did, but could not say. A dilemma, I suppose. They would not bow nor would I take their advice. No, not all. But what to do?"

"Yes bald man, what?"

"I withdrew. A little. At first. Only a little. But little rhymes with quitter, if you think about it. Then I quit a little more and had less power over them. Once I had a chair in my hand, another time a knife. Maybe they would have reported me, maybe not. Instead I just stood mostly, stood and let the tigers and bears and puppets prowl and prance. That's how I think of the whole episode, anyway. It got away from me, I suppose.

"It was going to be one of my last hunts. I was in the twilight of my safari days."

Macky started to struggle but the old man sent his tongue into Macky's ear.

"Look at the white pages looking at you. I have hunted down many an idea. Yet as distinguished as I am when you get to be my age you finally reflect on your accomplishments and drink yourself silly or smart, yet youth youth youth is all wasted on the young."

The old man started to sweat.

"I know a man who wrote small and large pieces about the underworld. He was one of those. Youth, they know they are young, they also know who is old, too, can smell an element in your bones, brain cells, your breath, and hair, and they translate that smell into 'Time's up old sir.'"

Macky's ear started to bleed a little.

"I couldn't keep up with them—you understand that I suppose. You also have things you cannot keep up with, like the bovine references, I suppose. The young have a way of looking through you even with your defenses up. Do they care? No they do not, sonny-boy, for they know the kingdom is through the aged! The doors to whizzdom and knowledge are through you and be damned if we of old age are going to let it go without a fight! Fine, until on one of your last real hunts, it all comes down.

"It was all over a carcass and I was all gone after that. Those animals. One beast after another pitching in to carve or save this buck. I was in my element I tell ya! My heart-paced skipped the pace off the chart.

"And this one bear tore into the fray to stop the commotion. In the clearing I saw this, then another bear jumping on two tigers that had taken to breaking the carcasses' back. Carnal rampage. It was not supposed to happen that way at the blue watering hole. Everyone had a turn in bringing an offering but this time more was on the line, then the damn fucking carcass jumps up with a two by four not willing to be put down. Whap! Whap! Oh shit! The tigers were having none of it though and I screamed AAAH Lordy Jesus I Can't Shoot My Gun It's Done Gone Soft I Can't Muster AND And and I am without the once loyal native. Some of them were on my side, some not, but they had no guns to give me."

Macky's still staring down.

"I was their leader. How could I have withdrawn and quit? But I did I did and ran oh for the love of goodness I ran. Please forgive my weakness. I will never be the great white hunter I killed to be. I ran then, ran into a deep bottle and stayed there until I dried up. Then the Èlegantes ate my pulpy fiber and drank my alcoholic fluids. Next, being remade, I was brought here."

The book went dark. The train stopped and the lights came back on, still showing empty seats benches up and down the cars.

The old man took his tongue out of Macky's ear and stared forward again. Color came back to the old man. He licked his lips; they having Macky's blood on them. The doors opened and Macky looked at the old man, wondering.

"I have to go now, son, board another car and tell my tale again, sonny. Remember my story and don't be like me. Don't you dare quit! If you do, when the Èlegantes come for you, you will be judged a non-hacker and brought here to stay."

The glove that housed Macky's hand crumbled away. Macky looked at it, remembered that he was being rude and decided to not say goodbye.

A Three Hour Tour

Macky wanted to think about the old man having to re-tell his story with such brevity. Plus the question of how deep underground they were. The smell was a chocolaty earth smell, now it was more of base metals, warm wet base metals. He looked through the opened doors and heard the shuffling of feet. Papers began to fall. More rumbling of feet stumbling, shuffling clearer voices. Confetti, champagne corks popped! Full reports, spreadsheets outside, feces, theses rained inside and out of the car. Macky squeezed under a bench. A group of ten circling a tall man came in. All in suit dress suits, pants suits, all the suits that professionals wear. A few had tambourines. One woman had a flute. A chipper, tall fellow broke away, and Tall-y went to stand next to Macky who had decided to come out from under the bench. On the car floor certificates and art degrees abounded. Tall-y had a tambourine and was banging it against his butt and shakin his hips. Bang bang bang bang three, two, one.

He sat.

"Hello and how do you do! Whew, I love to do that, I really do love to make noise. I am a very important man. But do not think I can help you. If you have a problem with anyone or anything do not count on me. Do it yourself. Yup, that's my belief. Even my second in command wouldn't tell you that. Plus the memo would take weeks to get to you."

Macky perplexed, "Is that all you have to say to me?"

"Oh no, not as a president. I am brought onboard to straighten things out, not lick boot."

"But—"

"But nothing young laddy!" Tall-y lifted his veils to look at the prestigious art degrees that littered the floor. The staff of Tall-y scrambled to grab the papers, eat the pages, and sweat the reams out of their pores. In Macky's ear, "I can never get away from them," then sitting up, "I will tell you why you should stand alone and not trust the group which appointed you."

"But I don't have a group."

"Not all groups are outside your head."

"Oh. Well—"

"I will tell you something that happened on my watch . . . not my fault mind you, but my watch.

"I'm a fetching prize you know. Then even more for I was mortal. All like me are valuable you know. My jaw my strong jaw, a full olive face with deep eyes. I am a handsome boy with a handsome man viewpoint of the important kind. Still got it!"

Tall-y is six-four, puffy chested square shouldered small waisted flat haired no facial hair nut. He is wearing four or five colored veils. No eyebrows. He is a black preacher funeral suit wearer.

"I liked giving speeches. I also liked that touch I got away with when the women wanted me to touch them. No they didn't. Yes they did. I could always get away with it for the women who didn't want it were in the minority. And the few who still stood offended, my people would do my battles and those would be gone. They needed me like that, yes?

"One day, one pretty blue day on the water I thought of my importance. It was on the rise. I am as then, a man—a self-made man. Then there was a splash. Man overboard is what you say but this time it was a woman.

"Anyway, she was on my yacht because she and all the new people had to come and meet me. They wanted me, needed me and I loved to be needed. And I was pretty. You know, even though we're from different places we're the same. True, I have pedigree and you are low class. I even went to an old school older than the one they attended. The jokers and you were schooled . . . hm, we don't have that much in common after all." Macky wondered why the train did not move. Finally it shuddered. Jerked. It began to move and as it did, so did the dancers of mirth. Tall-y stood erect, chest out.

"The woman bobbed up and down and I had a mission! Yes! I was in boat shoes while she had high heel shoes—I had always seen to that. It was such a pretty day, warm, jolly, and full of sweet meats and strong drink. Gin and juice. Gin and Juice, Gin and ice. Gin and ice. And in the end, just gin and gin and gin."

"Help me! I can't swim!"

"Woman overboard, auruga ahruga!"

Everyone on the yacht ran over to the starboard side and watched the junior assistant bob less and less. A life preserver was thrown to her. It hit her with a large amount of force, breaking her nose. The preserver was still shrink-wrapped in plastic. Her blood mixed with the ocean sending out the come and get it alarm to the fish with aggressive mouths. In the back of the crowd someone wondered if this president was insured.

The junior rose, bobbed fewer times as the trustees looked at their leader for direction.

"I, feeling their pain yelled, 'Stand back everyone, I won't smother her, I mean I'll save her!' Thus, instead of getting the small lifeboat I dived into the ocean forgetting of my own safety. Indeed, for I cannot swim."

Tall-y crouched down.

"I dog paddled over to her with that in mind and was pitched by the waves. Seeing the life preserver being clutched by her then not, then I, I . . . grabbed it away from her for dear life and watched her sink. I then bit and scratched my lovely face, all the while knowing those on board were drunk and decided not to see what was happening. I was thrown a line and pulled on board. Whew! I screamed at the gods for taking her under, all to the claps and cheers of the trustees. The others who were not as convinced but thought about liability also chimed in. Except for the one who wondered about insurance. She recorded the affair instead of clapping."

He stood erect again.

"The papers raved about it for weeks, this dashing Clark Kent type of guy being a real life Superman. I was celebrated. Why not? I made everyone look good in my bravery. They even told me so. I thought about it, a little, but balls! A medal plus a key to the city! All for having done what I did. Then the banquet to honor me."

He sat down and flipped the veils up to eyeball Macky. "I was about to utter my man of the month speech when on the ceiling, she who launched a life boat played what really happened." He lowered his veils.

"I left before the tape ended, went home and got my .45. I then called the trustees to the yacht. They arrived one by one., saying they would have to tell, but they still believed in me. Brought into the boardroom that way. Shot in that fashion. Then the Élegantes showed up and told me the consequences of being a shooter with promise. I am a man of some principle after all. I shot myself, but these Élegantes are contracted.

"Our punishment is to twirl papers around with me warning on the dangers of being too important without being true to the mission."

The train stopped. The doors opened. Tall-y got off, tambourine silent, head down. The trustees followed behind him. As the train started to move again Macky heard a tambourine rattling.

There's gold in them thar hills!

Macky closed his eyes. Napped. Opened his eyes. There were two large shadows, five cars down. As he walked towards them the metal floor turned into hardwood. The aluminum railings were now pig iron. Seats of hay instead of foam. The doors had to be hand cranked to be opened. He stopped at the sight of a colored woman in chains. The man holding her chains was in chains held by her. The man said he was a Cherokee man.

"I am tired, little one, but I please you sit down with me."

"Yes, sit," from the woman who wore shackles around her ankles and neck. "Oh these? They're what they are and this is what it is: he is trapped with me. He was a greedy ol fool. I own him now as he owned me then."

"She speaks the truth, son. Were those pants red at sometime? On the trail out of my homeland we were waiting at the Great River for a boat to take us across the known land and into barbarian territory. On the dock waiting, while I leaned over crying about my life, this one snuck up on me, wrapped these chains around me and pushed us into the water where we slept until the Èlegantes woke us by munching us up. They also put us in this coffin of steel wheels."

The woman, Rosetta, smiled and frowned. "I did to him what he did not do unto me. But by doing so I broke my word to my love. This has meant that I am his keeper till he learns."

Macky sat down across from the Cherokee guy with wet hair, blue veins everywhere with a mossy blanket around him and Rosetta of purple skin and a shawl. Neither one had eyes and their fingers were negligible. Macky asked about the lesson. She spoke up, "Listen to what happened to his people."

Macky began to change his mind when a warm fat breeze rose from the floor.

"For as long as I am sane," his thought went, "I will remember the air that took me away from aches, pains and Bad Dandy."

It also stopped him from seeing shadows of woolly mammoths goring stupid hunters further back on the train.

The breeze transported them back to Chief Sturges' people when they lived by themselves, traded, fought, and farmed. When the rumors of the bright eyed ones that wore metal skins to the south and west were still more conjecture than fact. And even brighter skinned ones who did not bathe everyday. The walls of the car expanded. Macky slowed his breathing as the train quieted. No bidah or bodoo sounds; the noise metal wheels make as they roll over rail-connectors. Now it was just the foolish.

"We were not worried about these new-eyed people. In the beginning those with the metal skins only came so far and no more, but those were not the same as the bleached ones. We were not as lucky when it came to those from the land of father fog and mother castle. We met them and talked for many summers. Dirty and rude but they had superior weapons and short tempers. We made peace.

"Some of us took to their ways, for they were not too different from our own. Fought on their side against the daughters and sons of father fog and mother castle. Those who were born further north than I. Places where there were no more turkey.

"The Born-here white eye won against their parents in a terrible battle. Some called it their independence. These younger ones did not respect their parents anymore and we prayed they would perish. We were assured this would work. Our gods would see to it. They did not. Our gods were not as strong as the flintlock and ball and powder and cannon. We were brave, but not immortal.

"We made peace with the Born-heres. Many more summers and winters past. Many chiefs of command. Andrew Jackson, I was in awe of him, this wild man with long wild white hair. I even smoked with him once. Though I could not see into his heart. None of us could. Our gods did not let us. Even they were afraid of the Born-heres. So we negotiated. We bought her people to show we could do business. We took to their god who was much stronger than ours. We created charters and helped the chief in command defeat the Creek. He loved us then but we still could not look into his heart. We did not understand his god."

Chief Sturges just looked ahead.

"We found ourselves surrounded by those we fought for and though we had assimilated they took our land. We were a sovereign. We debated in our great councils and council fires. We had to. But the victorious white eyes had found a drug called gold. This was a strong drug that could only be gotten from digging up the ground. The ground was then never put back after the drug was harvested. Many of the bright eyes turned rabid whenever a little touched them."

Rosetta shifted and smiled but stayed silent.

"Enough was never enough. Our land had a lot of gold. This drug was worth more than our children, values, way of life, even if we could do business. Some of us still did business, while drawing up land treaties that were similar to those chief of command Jackson said he was proud of. Finally we did more: we palavered with his great judges. His Supreme Court agreed with us, but chief in command Jackson did not. Neither did his people. They forced us to leave over land and water. What could we do? What did we have left? Slaves? A few provisions? We were lost. We were robbed of our culture. I think we lost our minds, too.

"That was our downfall. We should have made war from the beginning and stolen their guns. Killed their leaders and beheaded their children and taken all their women. Now that I have told you my story and hers, when you go from here remember to have me delivered from this. I am civilized now. Make the great new-eyed chief release me so I can go back to my land. I will buy more Black slaves if that is his wish. That is the lesson I am learning, yes?"

Rosetta looked at Macky, "That's why he will always be mine."

*   *   *

The car filled with scenes of crying and people falling dead along a dusty trail. Walls of wood with portraits of indigenous people came into view. The train rocked, slowed down and happened to rise. Macky stood up and walked back to his seat. At one point he looked back and did not see the portraits, the hardwood floors, the iron, none of it except Rosetta flipping him off.

After making it back to his seat Macky wondered if he should get off as the train leveled off again and slide to a stop. The door opened. A sign said all stupid cows needed to get the f off all trains.

III

The Promised Land

CHAPTER NINE

My, them handles is chased silver ain't they?

Sweeney Todd

1. THE TEACHER

Bad Dandy does not drive a car. Bad Dandy rides in a car with speakers in the dash. Speakers for car seats. A speaker for a steering wheel. The tires are made from the cones of speakers. The knobs are shrunken speakers. All the speakers help. They discharge white noise. White noise helps him focus. What he focuses on is a whisper. The whisper is repeated. "I am the greatest."

He's looking at the book of making, breathing slowly, feeling the liers board the train. This time Macky will not fail him. Macky will answer as a remembering cow.

Bad Dandy has a silvery sequenced shirt on. It's unbuttoned to his navel. The sleeves plumb at his wrists, cuff linked with 300-carat rubies. A ring of gold is on every finger. Zodiac trinkets are gently jingling between the triangle of plugged chest hair and his shirt. His hair is slicked back. He has sharpened his teeth. He's got wrap around glasses on with colored lenses. Drool, every now and again, trickles down his chin, staining the silk. A chalice by his feet. He is wearing stacks with spats. Black zoot pants. Plies in his back pocket.

The car glides to a stop. Bad Dandy is at the bottom of the hill. Glende opens his door. He stands at the bottom of the hill. Glende drapes a silver cape around him. He drops to one knee. Glende does the same. When they get up a breeze told them Macky's about to stare at the driver with the doll yelling something about his Hyundai Elantra.

Glende drives off thinking her favors for the one now known as Bad Dandy, later known as the Lunatic were done for now.

The Èlegantes have gotten into an automobile on its way to the station where Macky boarded. They are hoping he's been lazy so his flesh will be tender.

CHAPTER TEN

Be there in the morning

Michael Jackson

1. A NOD TO RONALD

Macky ran up the stairs instead of taking the escalator. It smelled of yellow and even more yellowed body fluids. At the top of the stairs a dice game was going on, almost blocking the entrance. Two were cops. His female partner was winning. Then again, he held his pistol in one hand and in the other held his partners'.

Macky ran out into the street and noticed the traffic. He noticed some crazed fool driving a polished Ford Festiva screaming, "Remember the Hyundai Elantra! Remember the Hyundai Elantra! Remember the Hyundai Elantra! YEHAAAAYYYY," and angling to clip the people on either sidewalk. They easily dodged his vehicle that kept sputtering and dying out. The driver had an orange doll that he was shaking at them. He also blared John Tesch as he aimed his car towards no one in particular talking about how civilization f'ed him up and new and decent phone sex was withheld. Ronald was also looking for the mouths of the Èlegantes. Macky thought about Ronald but could not take that into account.

As Macky ran away another a train pulled up. It was full of Èlegantes. The Èlegantes were coming after all.

2. FIGHTING THE GOOD FIGHT

Macky ran until his legs wobbled. He stopped then staggered into an alley. This was not one he was accustomed to; where he lived the alleys were mostly clean. He slid down the wall until his left hand rested in something chunky and gelatinous. Macky did not look at it, only wiped it off with a piece of sticky newspaper. Time to press on.

Back out on the sidewalk he saw women wearing spiked collars, hair and chaps. The men were doing the same. Some of them should have worn something under those chaps. Or at least tan. Or at least rented a "Buns of Steel" video. A tall man with long straight silver hair and silver Uncle Sam costume walked past him. Even Uncle's box was silver. Before long, without Uncle knowing which way or why they were coming, the Èlegantes would easily gobble him up.

This place was dirtier than he thought it would be. More than that, the dirt was given free ride on the wind and did witch dances around poles, cars, people. Stop signs and other traffic announcements like *Only MUNI is special and can turn here* were painted over. Dog, man, bird feces co-mingled on the sidewalks, even though there were an over abundance of street cleaning signs.

Homeless people abounded everywhere. Not the one or two you could blithely imagine were actually wealthy yet eccentric, but whole gypsy caravans. Macky thought he could make some real money if he could take some of these units back to the lab with him. Where he was from, they would pay a pretty penny for such cash cows. The thought about that stopped as he noticed a billboard.

The billboard said true believers fall to get up. That being so he found the tallest hill he could find and threw himself down it. Down the hill he went, tumbling bumping into men and women who needed to start showering again. He glanced up or what he thought was up and saw Èlegantes eating some meaty dirty people away. Macky thought up some poetry:

Vacancies. The wind makes the trash happy

makes the fleas in the trash happy gives disease

its cue to pounce

on me. I dodge the trash as best I can and

continue falling down the hill when Bad Dandy stops my roll.

They eyed each other but Macky couldn't help but notice there was a magnificent bridge in the background. A gray metal one and huge but it swayed. He squinted, thinking Bad Dandy was letting him see this. Bad Dandy was letting him look at gluttony and violence and nothingness. Did he think looking at the Èlegantes was the same as looking at lingerie on someone you want?

Macky would have looked forever if he could, if Bad Dandy hadn't begun shaking him.

"C'mon Elsie—!"

"Bad Dandy! The Èlegantes!"

"You still walk and talk full of chalk! Oh how the lactile fluid from the female of the bovine species is highly specific to the Nth degree in you!"

"I don't think I can do it, Bad Dandy. That's why I want to talk to you. That and the concrete mouths that are chasing me. Ya gotta help me!"

"Do you have an anvil from which you use to do your thinking, Elsie? It's got to be that! Want to know why? I've been aiding your Holstein ass since coming to you in your dreams but no more. Now when the Èlegantes get here they will devour your present existence. They will spit out a new you. Then you can help me carve the little prey and you know what? Huh? You will be just like me. You won't be me of course, you could never be that, but close. That's the job. And what comes after? Home. And with that comes Frenchie. Isn't that wonderful?"

Macky shook his head then body. "I only wanted Frenchie. I maybe wanted to meet you. I didn't want . . . I did, but you aren't—" and Bad Dandy smacked Macky with a slab of concrete. Macky slowly got to his knees.

"Cow. You buttermilk spewing cow! You take up my time and energy and now when you smell the barbecue grill you claim you're a vegan? Do you think that's how it works?"

Macky was a little more than halfway up when Bad Dandy kicked him in the mouth. Macky's head flipped back so far that his mouth lodged in the grass. He trembled and seizures flared. The jolt panicked the primordial in him and he thought whose house this is. He got up slowly, shaking, but when he did stand, now several feet back from Bad Dandy, he found a more diplomatic approach.

"I know you have helped me. You, you always have. I know you didn't have to and I'm grateful, Bad Dandy. You are a warrior who could have shirked his duty and been a great lounge singer. I have known that since dream three. But I am no performer. Yet you help the weak-kneed like myself find adventure and romance. You are superior to me, though this is not my lot; to serve in this war. I am flesh and weak and you transcend the corporal. You have tried with me, oh lord have you. I am such a sorry being."

Crumbled rushes cascaded. Concrete buildings did belly flops onto the streets. Rumble. Birds cawed. Deep in the ground and foothills the Èlegantes were eating the bottoms out of everything. Everything. From where they have come nothing was left. Light bent into blackness. Wonderful, yes?

3. COMING UP FOR AIR

The Èlegantes came up for air and zeroed in on Macky but stopped. Was he fighting with Bad Dandy? Pleading? Was Macky telling Bad Dandy they had not eaten him yet? They were wondering here, anxious, even. They had not eaten him before he got to this place, and knew there could be repercussion for things done out of turn. The Èlegantes have been known to go soft.

Once they were eating away, doing their duty, when they came up on an old woman. They circled this bag lady, drooling at the texture of her muscles, which looked loose and limp, even from the outside. They did not touch her. Twelve just circled her. Then another twelve and on until a wall was built around her. Èlegantes that had just come from gobbling up bags of gold coin spate those bags at her feet. Then three others spate up chunks of sidewalk out of where they had eaten to a part of the future where they would not be until now, if they lived that long. But she was just a bag lady. Tired, wrinkled, struggling, wearing three jackets too small. Soiled pants, mismatched shoes and stringy gray hair teased out of a dirty green beret with the name "Glende" sewn in.

She put the bags of coins in her shopping cart along with a bat and took the road to the future. They then went back to work, wondering if anybody would tell, wondering what would be the repercussions.

Right before they were going to gobble her down she reached into her buggy and brought out that dented aluminum Louisville slugger. With her other hand, holding it close to her chest, was an itty-bitty kitty, meowing and licking her chin.

4. OBJECTION TO A GOOD WAR

"I refuse to recite the answer to 'How's the cow' until you present Frenchie!"

Bad Dandy gave Macky a blow to the gut then an upper cut that Macky thought he was going to be able to block then counter-punch. He almost did, a little, before staggering back giving Bad Dandy a good look to where to throw dirt into Macky's eyes. Bad Dandy then picked Macky up and threw him down. Macky's hip fractured a little. Macky laid on his back very still. His eyes burned. Bad Dandy sat on him and spat in Macky's face, making mud there. Bad Dandy fetched the pair of pliers from his back pocket. Macky double clamped his mouth shut but Bad Dandy squeezed Macky's balls until the cells started to give.

"Cows and monkeys have no need for wisdom teeth, that's what I say. Is that true? Answer quick for I think a sunset death would be nice for one Bad Tooth in particular."

The pliers went in a little. A little more, having forced themselves into Macky's mouth, past his front teeth and not bothering with the combative tongue. The metal teeth griped Bad Tooth, which throbbed for protection.

"Shed wauff she talks—"

"You ungrateful coward. You incorrigible bovine munching pleasing monkey weak fuck. I tried to show you the way to frenchie and this is what I get? You think she likes milk and oatmeal? Do you understand me boy? Predators! All the way. How can I prove to Lucky Time that I can be a God if I cannot turn one pathetic fuck into a killer?" Dandy paused to remember what Macky mumbled. A twinkle in his eyes and satisfaction wrinkled his lips. He also removed the pliers and the right hand on Macky's sack. Macky curled into a ball.

"Good good, you know who is all-powerful: The teacher. I will get off you even, in a minute that is. We will also pause the rest of your training. Maybe. If the Èlegantes decide not to eat some of you. But all of this is contingent on you being decisive, making decisions and standing by them. You will have to say something in the morning, in other words. If not, it will be nothing but painful delights."

Bad Dandy brought his toolbox down on Macky's chest. Macky spat out blood while Bad Dandy helped him up. Bad Dandy looked for an answer. Macky nodded yes. Bad Dandy open palm slapped Macky across the eyes. In one, blood leaked. Bad Dandy gave a retrench salute to the Èlegantes. Bad Dandy knew that he had little breathing room but just a little: The Èlegantes were always saps for bag ladies. As for Macky, he was not at the next phase, but it was close. Real close.

"By all that is good, you are finally getting somewhere. A little. Come with me to my house and I will prepare you for going back for more training."

"But I don't—" And sees the Èlegantes still frozen. They looked amazed that Macky had gotten this far and wonder what will happen if he is not gobbled down next time.

"Yes, Bad Dandy. Take me to your house, sir.

Macky does not see them leave one by one.

In the morning Dandy was still smiling.

"I still decided to carve up your little friend. Curious George is hanging from the hanging rope and his heart, now purple and cold is sewn into his right hand with his throat slashed, filled with stuffing and in his left hand, his lungs. He said for you to go fuck yourself. I deplore such language, but they were his last words and he did die in vain. For more happy news you still don't have what it takes so you go back to get refocused. You already knew that though. What you do not know though is that you are moving closer to how you should be and that I'm proud. Yesterday with the Èlegantes chasing you, you denied me. That is something to build upon."

"But I loved George."

"Oh don't be so easy, idiot. I didn't slice the monkey up last night, I did it awhile ago. If you hadn't stood up to me there would have been a problem, huh? But besides working on a more efficient weapon, work on not being so gullible."

"What about working on Frenchie? Or a little painkiller?"

Bad Dandy slapped and kicked him in the ribs. Smiling, leaning over Macky, "There you go for painkiller! As for meeting Frenchie why of course not. To meet her you must already have the job, the house, and well on the way to making something of yourself. You are no way even close to having the job part down, silly goose."

Clutching his chest and making it to his knees, "But in the dreams you showed me a picture of her. You said it was from her. That she has seen me and thought me cute."

"That was when you had promise. Through pain, Macky, you hve potential. That's why you are going back, for if you are not ready to recognize the power of fear in a handful of dust, then through pain I will teach you honor. Now, how's the cow?"

"Sir, she walks, she talks, she's full of chalk. The lactile fluid from the female of the bovine species is highly prolific to the nth degree, sir."

5. GETTING BACK IN THE WAR

It is raining. Macky is crying on the outside, but smiling inside. He is also back, been shipped back to the lab. His crate bumped against one smuggling himself from Down South going North. But Macky did not take that into account.

Diary entry

Dear diary, I am back on the IV drip. They got me back up to the 300 plus pounds. Wait, no, I'm back down. It's the drugs, they make me lose perspective. Things have flip-flopped, switches turned on and off, back and forth, since I was young. But I still love her. But I need Jenny Craig, or maybe some of that Dick Gregory. My heart needs a helper to keep going but not because I'm seven foot, dig me? My heart is bigger than the body it's in. Plus it's sluggish. It doesn't matter, I'm talking out of sorts. I'm no longer 300 pounds, remember?

So, I guess no Gregory. I wonder what will happen when I dream this time.

CHAPTER ELEVEN

It was the monster mash

Bobby Pickett

1. REVING THE MOTOR

Frenchie is pacing. "Everyday I get sicker and sicker and puke and squat. This life with the labcoaters is not going to be for me. I will escape. Come back. And kill everyone who has been aided by the tests run on me."

She did, for her cage opened the way Macky's did. Liberated on the same day. She now having broken into a car—with the head of the driver, sped away.

"A breeder, a breeder they said! Wind chimes, grass, running water, what are those things to me! Are they a few of my favorite things? No, but meat and milk are. The lactile fluid from the female of the bovine species is highly prolific to the nth degree, sir! Oh how the folk will suffer but only those who are supposed to be killers and have decided to stray from the mission. And they will not be able to recite the forget lines: Sir, my cranium consisting of Vermont marble, volcanic lava, and African ivory, covered with a thick layer of case hardened steel, forms an impenetrable barrier to all that seek to impress itself upon the ashen tissues of my brain. Hence, the effulgent and ostentatiously effervescent phrases just directed and reiterate for my comprehension have failed to penetrate and permeate the somniferous forces of my atrocious intelligence. To arms to arms, and I will be known as someone else without definition. But what is the definition of leather? 'If the fresh skin of an animal, cleaned and divested of all hair, fat, and other extraneous matter, be immersed in a dilute solution of tannic acid, a chemical combination ensues; the gelatinous tissue of the skin is converted into a non-putrescible substance, impervious to and insoluble in water; this, sir, is leather.

But I will be known as Grace.

www.ingramcontent.com/pod-product-compliance
Lightning Source LLC
Chambersburg PA
CBHW031605260626
47154CB00020B/1599